Mummified Meringues

Leighann Dobbs

This is a work of fiction.

None of it is real. All names, places, and events are products of the author's imagination. Any resemblance to real names, places, or events are purely coincidental, and should not be construed as being real.

Cover art by: http://www.coverkicks.com

Chapter One

Lexy Baker-Perillo took a bite of the chocolate meringue cookie and let the carefully crafted confection melt in her mouth.

Needs more sugar, she thought, as she looked around the basement of the 1950s ranch-style home where she and her husband, Jack Perillo, were sorting through the decades of accumulation that cluttered every inch of the small area. They'd been working on organizing the items off and on for months and it seemed like they'd barely made any progress.

But, they needed to get a move-on because Jack didn't want to put the house on the market until the basement was cleaned out and Lexy dearly wanted to sell the house soon so she could pay back the loan her parents had given her to start her bakery, *The Cup and Cake*.

"Why can't we just sell the house with all this stuff in it?" Lexy asked.

Jack looked up from the box he'd been digging in and straightened, his head almost brushing the low ceiling. He rubbed his hand down his stubble-dotted chin and turned his velvety brown eyes on Lexy.

"Because," he said as he walked toward her. "No one buys a house that comes with a basement full of stuff."

"*You* did," she pointed out as she watched him pick a meringue cookie from the plate.

Jack's lopsided grin made her smile. He leaned over and placed a gentle kiss on the tip of her nose that made her heart flutter. "That was just so I could get close to *you*."

Jack was joking, of course. He hadn't known she lived behind him when he bought the house, but the memory of their first meeting warmed Lexy's heart. She'd bought her house from her grandmother, Nans, who had decided she'd have more fun living in the new retirement center in town where most of her friends were. The house was right behind Jack's, with backyards separated by an old fence.

One night, Lexy's Shih-Tzu poodle mix, Sprinkles, had slipped through a gap in the fence and proceeded to do her nightly business in Jack's neatly manicured shrubs. Much to Lexy's embarrassment, Jack had come out to see who was skulking around in his garden and that's how they'd first met.

Of course, she'd had no idea Jack was a homicide detective or that she would soon become his number one suspect in the murder of her ex-boyfriend, but thankfully, things had eventually worked out and now they were married with neighboring houses. They'd decided to take up residence in Lexy's house since she had so many childhood memories there and Jack's was going to be put up for sale ... that is, if they ever got the basement done.

Jack bit into the cookie and headed back into the maze of boxes.

"These need more sugar if you expect to win that dessert contest," he shot over his shoulder as he disappeared from view.

Lexy tapped her finger on the top of the box she was supposed to be sorting. The dessert contest was a yearly event in Brook Ridge Falls. Each year the town held a contest based on a certain type of dessert or dessert ingredient. One year it was chocolate, and another year it was pecans. This year, it was meringue.

Lexy sighed and plucked at the folded-over lid of the box. She'd much rather be in her bakery perfecting her meringue cookie recipe and thinking up interesting variations than in here, looking at more than fifty years of old stuff that was left in the basement by the previous owner. Winning the contest could give her business important publicity.

"Woof!"

"Sprinkles, come here." Lexy craned her neck in the direction of Sprinkles' bark which, near as she could tell, came from the far corner of the room.

"Woof!"

Scratch, scratch, scratch.

"What is she doing?"

"Probably just exploring." Jack's muffled voice came from inside a box he was inspecting, and then he added, "Hey, check this out."

Lexy looked up to see him holding up a vintage, jadeite green triple-head milkshake mixer. "That's kind of neat. Does it work?"

"Don't know, but this place is full of retro kitchenware."

"And other stuff," Lexy mumbled as she flipped up the lid. Leaning to look in, her shoulder length, mink-brown hair fell across the side of her face and she shoved it behind her ear impatiently. A pungent whiff of mildew drifted into her nostrils as she peered in at a box full of musty linens.

"It's a treasure trove of nostalgia."

"Woof!"

Scratch.

"Nans said all the items might add to the appeal of the house for a new buyer." Lexy waved her hand around the room. "They could practically outfit the whole house with everything they need just from the items in here."

Jack wrinkled his brow at her. "I'm not sure what's with Nans. She told me that, too, but the real estate agent was pretty clear that having the basement full like this would make the house hard to sell. Besides, some of this stuff is valuable. We could sell it and make even more money."

Scratch, scratch, scratch, scratch.

"Woof! Woof!"

"Sprinkles, cut it out!" Lexy felt a tingle of nerves.

What was that dog into?

Jack brought a box up to the front of the room where they'd decided to pile up the 'sellable' items. Space was at a premium in the tightly packed basement and he had to shuffle sideways to get past her and into the designated area.

"You're going to have to go a little faster if you want to finish this any time soon," he said.

"Right." Lexy closed up the box and slid it over to the 'trash' area—the linens were too musty to be of any good to anyone. "It's just that it takes so much time to go through this stuff, I'm not sure it will be worth it."

"Woof! Woof!"

Lexy spun around, trying to hone in on Sprinkles barks. "Can you see where she is? I hope she isn't stuck somewhere."

Scratch, scratch, scratch.

"It sounds like she's down in the back corner." Jack started toward the corner.

"Woof!"

"Sprinkles. Come to Mommy." Lexy tried to coax her out into the open. "We may never find her in this mess."

Scratch, scratch, scratch.

"I'm sure we can lure her out with a treat." Jack yelled the last word to catch the dog's attention but Sprinkles didn't stop digging.

Lexy's anxiety grew as Sprinkles' digging took on a feverish pace and she followed Jack toward the sound.

"Sprinkles, stop!"

"Woof!"

Scratch, scratch, Smash!

"Yipe!"

Lexy's heart stuttered when she heard the dog's yelp and she frantically shoved boxes aside to get to Sprinkles.

Jack got there first, and by the time Lexy cleared the last box, she found him staring at a hole in the wall. Chunks of cement lay at his feet. Sprinkles looked up at them as if she'd just accomplished some sort of intricate trick and was awaiting her reward. The dog's white fur was covered with gray dust and Lexy might have laughed if she wasn't so concerned about the hole in Jack's foundation wall.

"Sprinkles!" Lexy admonished the dog, then put her hand on Jack's arm. "Jeez, Jack I'm sorry about that hole. I don't know what got into her."

Jack bent down and looked into the hole. "This isn't right."

"I know. Sprinkle's has never done anything like that." Lexy gave the dog a sharp look, her heart melting a little at the dog's obvious pride in her destructive work. "I'll pay to get it fixed right away."

"No, not that." Jack reached out and pulled another chunk of cement away. "This should be the foundation wall with dirt behind it, but it looks like there's a space behind here."

Lexy furrowed her brow. "A space?"

"Yeah." Jack stood and looked down the length of the wall, then up at the ceiling, then turned and looked around the basement. "I never really looked around down here, but it seems like this wall is a bit shy of the outer edge of the house and there's another section behind it."

Lexy's eyes swept the length of the wall. "But there's no door or anything."

"That's what's so strange about it. It's all sealed to make it look just like the other walls."

"Like a secret room?" Lexy asked.

"Exactly." Jack bent down and pulled at a loose chunk of cement, then peered through the hole again. "It's dark in there. Can you get the flashlight?"

The sounds of Jack breaking away bits of cement accompanied Lexy as she wove her way through the boxes to the front to retrieve the large flashlight they'd left by the steps.

"Why would they have a secret room in here?" Lexy asked as she made her way back. She crouched down beside him and handed him the light.

Jack had worked a two-foot opening in the wall. He shined the light inside to reveal a narrow space, about two feet, wide running the length of the wall.

"I have no idea," he said as he poked his face into the hole and played the light slowly down the entire length of the space.

Lexy stuck her face in beside his and the smell of must, dry earth and something else she couldn't quite place tickled her nose. She felt a pang of disappointment—the room appeared to be empty. And then the flashlight revealed something in the far corner.

Lexy grabbed Jack's arm. "Wait. What's that?"

"What?" Jack aimed the beam of light into the corner.

"Oh, it's just a sack of old, rotted potatoes," Lexy said as she looked at the bottom of the brown sack laying like a lump in the corner. Some potatoes must have fallen out and were lying in small, dirty lumps around it.

"Wait a minute ..." Jack angled the flashlight on the sack and Lexy realized the brown, leathery form was too long to be a sack of potatoes and not only that, it appeared to be wearing a pair of shorts, a wife beater t-shirt and one red flip-flop on its right foot.

Jack let the light linger at the top of the 'sack' and Lexy's heart jerked in her chest when she recognized that it was a face.

She grabbed Jack's arm, her green eyes wide. "Is that what I think it is?"

"I'm afraid so." Jack's face turned grim. "We've got a mummy in our basement."

***

Lexy took a step backwards, bumping into a box and almost falling over it as horror spread through her. Her mind flashed on all of the candlelight dinners, romantic evenings, and relaxing nights watching TV upstairs in Jack's house ... and the whole time, a dead body had lain down here in this secret room.

"How long has it been here?" she asked.

Jack shrugged. "I have no idea. I guess at least since before I bought the place, because I sure as heck didn't seal it up in there."

Jack paced to the corner and moved a stack of boxes aside to inspect the joint where the walls met. "It looks like someone built that false wall to make the secret room. That wall is wood frame construction, not cinderblock like the rest of the foundation. Then they refinished it just like the other walls on purpose, so no one would even know the room was there. It's so narrow that I don't think you'd know unless you measured the room. If it wasn't for Sprinkles, we might never have noticed it."

"So someone did this on purpose?"

Jack looked at her and nodded. "There's no way this was an accident."

Lexy shivered, then bent down to peek into the room again. She'd seen quite a few dead bodies in her time, but never one that was mummified. It looked so strange, with the leathery skin stretched tight and the clothing, although dirty and a bit worse for the wear, still on it. "I can't believe someone put a person in here, sealed them up and left them to die."

"Maybe they were already dead."

"Well, that's a slightly more pleasant thought." Lexy shuddered, realizing there had been a killer loose in the neighborhood and right in the house behind Nans. Of course, given Nans' odd hobby of investigating murders, Lexy realized that the older woman would have probably been more intrigued than repulsed.

She made a mental note to call her grandmother right away. This must have happened when Nans was living in the house behind Jack, and Lexy was sure her grandmother wouldn't be able to resist investigating the death that had happened practically right under her nose. "How long does it take for a body to mummify and why didn't it deteriorate into a skeleton?"

"That's a good question. I guess it must have been pretty dry in there. I don't know how long the process takes, but I think mummies can be preserved for centuries like this." Jack bent down with his face near the hole and sniffed. "What's that strange smell?"

"Mummy smell?"

"No, something else. It smells flowery."

Lexy bent down closer to the hole and inhaled deeply. Her nose picked up on that familiar scent again and then she realized what it was. "Hmmm, that's weird. Let me see that flashlight."

Jack handed the flashlight over and Lexy aimed it at the small lumps beside the body that she'd *thought* were potatoes.

"Ahhh, so that explains it," she said.

Jack frowned at her. "Explains what?"

"See those small lumps?" Lexy trained the flashlight on one of the lumps. "I thought they were potatoes but now I can see they are sachets."

Jack let out an exasperated sigh. "And exactly what is a sachet?"

"It's a little pouch that you can put dried flowers and scents in. Ladies used to use them in their lingerie drawer to add a nice smell. It's pretty old fashioned. I don't think anyone does it anymore. These are lavender-scented."

Jack's left brow ticked up. "And why do you think lavender sachets would be in here with a mummified body?"

"I'm guessing they put them in to hide the smell."

"Hide the smell?" Jack snorted. "It's pretty hard to hide the stench of a dead body. I don't think a few silky pouches of flowers is gonna do it, but I guess someone who wasn't so familiar with dead bodies might think so."

"So, you think this is the work of an amateur?"

Jack shrugged. "Hard to tell until we find out who the victim is. That's a job for the police. I guess I better put in the call."

Jack dug in his pocket with one hand and turned Lexy toward the exit with the other. "In the meantime, I guess we won't be continuing our work in the basement—this is a crime scene now."

They headed toward the exit with Sprinkles following obediently behind them. As they started up the stairs, Lexy looked back over her shoulder at the hole. "I wonder what horrible thing that person did to deserve the fate of being sealed up inside the basement wall."

"Good question." Jack speed dialed the police department. "But an even better question is ... *who* sealed them up in there and why?

Chapter Two

Lexy's mind whirled with questions as they waited on the front steps for the police. "You don't think those nice old people that lived here before you killed that person, do you?"

"The McDonalds?" Jack scrunched his face up. "I doubt it. They were just a nice, elderly couple and they certainly didn't act as if they were offloading a house with a mummy in the basement. I think it's more likely it was the builder."

"So you think the builder had a body to hide and made a secret room for it in the basement? That seems like the timing would have had to be perfect. Wouldn't someone have noticed that the foundation was off?"

Jack shrugged. "Maybe, but the space is so narrow that I doubt anyone would have noticed because the walls looked exactly the same from the inside."

"But why would a builder have a dead body?" Lexy wondered, then attempted to answer her own question. "Maybe the builder was mixed up with organized crime ... or maybe he took a payoff to hide bodies in his basements. Maybe all the homes in the neighborhood have a secret room with a mummy in them."

Jack laughed. "I doubt it's anything like that."

Lexy pressed her lips together. "Why *did* the McDonalds leave all their stuff, anyway? I mean it seems to me that would be a perfect way to discourage anyone from going near that back wall."

"During the final walkthrough for the house, I went in the basement and it was as full as it is now." Jack said. "The McDonalds seemed very embarrassed that they hadn't been able to get the stuff out in time. They were overwhelmed and moving to a senior assisted living place with no room for any of it. Charlie had a bad hip and couldn't even go in the basement. They had no kids and no one to help them haul it out. I took pity on them and said they could leave it and I'd deal with it."

Lexy's heart flooded with warmth at Jack's compassionate gesture. "Aww, that was sweet."

She pecked Jack on the cheek and smiled, noticing his neck turn an embarrassing shade of pink. It wasn't often that the tough detective let people see his softer side, but Lexy knew it was there.

Her happy feeling didn't last long, though, because seconds later, a caravan of Brook Ridge Falls Police cars pulled up. Detective Watson Davies catapulted out of the lead car and stormed in their direction. She stood staring down at them, her hands on the hips of her tight, black jeans. Lexy noticed she was wearing a black t-shirt with BFPD stamped in large white letters. The shirt was tucked into her jeans, which sported a gleaming gold badge clipped at her hip.

Lexy's stomach took a dive. She'd hoped that Jack's best friend and partner, John Darling, would be investigating. It figures they'd get Davies. Lexy had worked with Davies a few times in the past. Well, 'worked *with*' wasn't exactly right, more like worked *against*. Though to be fair, Davies had always shown she was interested in making sure justice was served. She and Lexy had had a somewhat adversarial relationship even though Davies had redeemed herself with a few random acts of kindness, and the diminutive detective did seem to have a tight bond with Nans.

Davies tilted her head at Lexy. "I got a call about a mummy ... this is a joke, right?"

Lexy shook her head.

"I should have known such a call would have something to do with you, Mrs. Baker-Perillo."

"It really doesn't have anything to do with Lexy." Jack put his arm around Lexy's shoulders and pulled her next to him. "She just happened to be here helping me. The body is in my basement."

Davies raised a perfectly plucked brow at Jack and he shrugged.

"Come on in and I'll show you." Jack stood up, pulling Lexy with him.

Davies motioned to the crime scene techs, who had been taking various pieces of equipment out of the cars behind her, and they all trudged into the house.

Davies looked up at Jack. "Seriously, Perillo, if this is a joke ..."

Jack raised his palm. "No joke, I swear."

They filed through the living room into the kitchen. Jack pointed to the basement door and gestured for Davies and her entourage to go down first.

"Jeez, Perillo, what are you, some kind of hoarder?" Davies stood at the bottom of the stairs, looking out over the fully packed basement.

"No. Actually, all of this is from the people who lived here before me. We were trying to sort it out so we can sell the house."

Davies' eyes fell on the plate of meringue cookies and she glanced over at Lexy. "Are these yours?"

Lexy nodded. "Help yourself."

Davies picked up a small cookie and shoved it in her mouth, screwing up her face as she chewed.

"Needs sugar," Davies mumbled around the mouthful of cookie, then swallowed, brushed off her fingers and looked around the basement. "Now, where, exactly, is this mummy?"

"Over here." Jack led them to the back wall and pointed at the hole.

Davies held out her hand, palm up, without saying a word and one of the crime unit techs slapped a flashlight into it. She squatted down, level with the hole, and aimed the light inside.

"It's on the right," Jack said.

Davies adjusted her aim. "Holy cow, I guess there really is a mummy in here. Never seen one of these before."

She pulled her head out and looked at Jack. "So, how do you figure it got in here?"

Jack shrugged. "I have no idea, but if you look at the wall, you can see someone took great care to make this false wall look like it was the end of the basement. It matches the intersecting walls perfectly."

Davies picked her way over to the corner, inspecting the walls with her flashlight. They were covered in a cement coating but Lexy knew from the outside of the house that the basement was actually made from cinderblocks. Inside, the coating gave it a more finished look—that of cement or stucco.

Davies ran her hand along the wall. "Right. I see it's cinderblock but plastered over. Do you think that was on purpose to make this little room?"

"I have no idea," Jack said.

"How long have you lived here?"

Jack scrunched his face and looked at the ceiling. "I think it's going on five years now."

"Bodies can mummify in less than a year under the right conditions," Davies mused.

A crime scene tech interrupted their conversation. "You don't expect us to climb in there, do you?" he asked, pointing to the small hole.

Jack shook his head. "No, I guess we'll have to widen the opening. But be careful not to disturb the area in back. Get some plastic bags and I'll help you widen it. We'll put the cement we remove in the bags so we can do forensic testing on the pieces later, and then let's—"

"Hold on there!" Davies held her hands up, palms out, and scowled at Jack.

"What?" Jack's brows creased as he looked from Davies to the hole to the crime scene techs.

"*I'm* the one in charge here, so *I'll* give the orders," Davies said.

Jack's brows shot up. "Well, you're only in charge because it's my day off. Tomorrow, I'll take over and —"

"Sorry, Jack. I don't think you'll be taking over. In fact, I'm going to have to ask you to leave the crime scene area."

"What? Why?"

"You can't investigate a crime in your own basement. Conflict of interest. And besides, right now, you're the number one suspect."

Chapter Three

Jack and Lexy retreated to her house where they peered out the kitchen window and through the backyards, anxiously trying to see what was going on at Jack's. They couldn't see what was happening inside, but they did manage to see the police bringing bags of what they assumed were pieces of concrete and other evidence out through the bulkhead door that faced Lexy's house.

Suddenly, as they watched, Sprinkles catapulted out of the basement with an angry Davies running up the bulkhead steps behind her.

Sprinkles bounded through the gap in the fence. Davies stopped just short of it when she spied Lexy and Jack looking out the window.

"Keep your dog out of here!" Davies yelled, her harsh words coming through the screen loud and clear.

"Sorry!" Lexy grimaced as she opened the screen door to the kitchen to let Sprinkles in.

"Bad dog," Lexy admonished Sprinkles half-heartedly. She had to admit she didn't feel all that bad that the dog had gotten Davies all riled up. But her joy in angering Davies was short-lived when she noticed something was wrong with Sprinkles. The dog held her head down and emitted a muted bark through clenched teeth.

"What's the matter, Sprinks?" Lexy bent down to get a closer look.

"What is it?" Jack asked.

"I don't know. She's acting kind of funny." Lexy looked up at Jack with worried eyes. "I hope she didn't catch some kind of mummy disease down there."

Sprinkles whined and wagged her tail, then spit something out on the floor.

"What's this?" Lexy picked up the small, dirty white piece of paper.

"Looks like a receipt," Jack said.

Lexy frowned at the light purple print. It was barely legible, but she could make out the name at the top. "It's from *The Elms Pub*."

"The bar down the street?" Jack asked, referring to the neighborhood bar a couple of streets over. It was named after the section of town they lived in which had been dubbed "The Elms" because of the large elm trees that lined the streets. The bar had been there for decades. Lexy always thought of it as the unofficial marker where the suburban neighborhood met the more commercial section of town.

"Yes, and judging by the prices, it looks pretty old." Lexy looked up at him. "Do you think we should give it to Davies?"

Jack shrugged. "Why? I'm sure Davies wouldn't let Sprinkles near that room, so it has nothing to do with the mummy. Sprinkles could have snagged that from any part of the basement."

"True. That place was pretty full."

"Woof!" Sprinkles wagged her tail and looked at Lexy. Forgetting about the receipt, Lexy went back to inspecting the dog, a feeling of relief spreading over her when she realized Sprinkles seemed fine.

"I don't even know how Sprinkles got in there, but I'm going to make sure she stays locked in here with us. I don't want her getting into anything more serious than an old receipt over there." Lexy gave the dog one final pat and stood holding the receipt up to Jack. "If you don't think this is a clue or anything important, I guess I'll just toss it out."

Jack nodded and turned his attention back out the window. "I just hope Davies knows what to do with the real clues if she finds them."

Lexy's heart twisted at the concerned look in Jack's eye.

"I'm sorry you can't investigate," she said, rubbing his back to soothe him.

Jack sighed. "Yeah, I hate that. I mean, Davies is okay, but I certainly don't want to turn something as important as this over to her."

"You don't think she really thinks you did it, do you?"

"Nah. It's logical that I would be the prime suspect now. The homeowner is exactly who I would suspect. I just hope she doesn't screw up or take too long to investigate because it could hold up the sale of the house."

"Oh." Lexy nervously nibbled one of the cookies she'd rescued when Davies had kicked them out of the house. She was counting on the house sale to go through soon. She needed the money to pay back her parents who were traveling the country in an RV after selling their home. Though her parents hadn't asked her to speed up the payments, she knew the RV needed repairs and she didn't want her parents to break down on the road—especially since she knew they couldn't afford to fix it because *she* owed them money.

"So, what are you going to do?" she asked.

"Oh, I can still investigate. I just might need a little help." Jack smiled at her and slid his arm around her shoulder. "Lucky thing I have my own amateur sleuth and her grandmother who I'm sure will be willing to check things out for me."

Lexy's lips curled in a smile. Usually, Jack got mad when she tried to investigate murders, but the last couple of times he'd seemed a lot more laid back about it. And now he was giving her permission to go digging around in the investigation.

She bubbled with excitement, then felt a tug of uncertainty. She was getting almost as bad as Nans when it came to wanting to explore crimes, and this was a big responsibility considering Jack was the primary suspect. Jack was putting his trust in her.

What if she screwed up?

"So, what do you say? Are you with me?" Jack's question pulled her out of her thoughts.

"Of course!" Lexy shook off her feelings of self-doubt. She could do this, especially with the help of her grandmother. Nans and her three friends, Ruth, Ida and Helen, were experienced amateur sleuths with a good track record. They'd solved several crimes and had worked with the police on a few cases. They were highly respected and even had a name for themselves, *The Ladies' Detective Club*. People had even started to seek their counsel as private investigators. If anyone could figure out who put the mummy in Jack's basement, it was Nans and the ladies.

"I'll call Nans and get her working on this right away. I know she'll want in on this." Lexy grabbed her phone off the kitchen table and dialed.

"Lexy, dear, how are you?"

"Great! I have some exciting news."

There was a moment of silence and then Nans ventured, "You're pregnant?"

Lexy scrunched her face up. "No, something even better. There's been a murder and we need to help Jack investigate it."

"Oh, really?" Nans voice was infused with interest. "The ladies didn't mention any new murders." Nans, Ruth Ida and Helen always seemed to know when there was a new crime of interest in town.

"That's because it just happened ... well, sort of." Lexy told her how they had discovered the mummy when cleaning out Jack's basement. "Isn't that great?"

Silence crackled in Lexy's ear. She held the phone out and looked at the display. Still connected. "Nans?"

"Sorry, dear," Nans said. "You were breaking up. Did you say something about your mother? I know she's been having trouble with the RV."

Lexy's stomach twisted—another reason for her to find the killer and close the case so the house could be sold. "No. I said we found a mummified body sealed up in Jack's basement."

"Sorry ... *crackle crackle* ... nection ... bad. We'll have to talk tomorrow. I'm running out for the night and will be busy until tomorrow afternoon ... *crackle ... crackle*."

And then the line went dead.

"What was that all about? Is she going to help?" Jack asked.

"Yeah, I guess so. I think we just had a bad connection so I'm not sure she heard what I was saying."

"Oh. Well, I'm sure she'll want to help. I can't picture her not wanting to investigate a juicy crime that happened right in her backyard."

"Right. Of course, she will. I'll fill her in tomorrow when we have a better connection." Lexy stared at the phone in her hand. Nans must not have been able to hear what she was saying, otherwise she was sure the older woman would have ditched all her plans and come straight over. But Nans had put her off until tomorrow afternoon.

The connection *must* have been bad—Lexy had even heard the crackling ... except the crackling seemed oddly familiar. It sounded just like the 'crackling' that sometimes happened when Lexy wanted to cut the phone conversations with her mother short. The ones she manufactured by crinkling candy bar wrappers next to the phone and dropping words on purpose.

Lexy never realized how much that sounded like real static because the static on the phone call with Nans must have been real. Otherwise, that would mean that Nans was using the same trick Lexy used … and why would Nans want to crinkle candy bar wrappers to fake a bad connection?

***

"I don't know why Nans isn't answering." Lexy frowned at her phone, then slipped it into the pocket of her vintage, rose pattern apron.

"Maybe she's just busy," her bakery assistant, Cassie, said without looking up from her task of frosting a three-tier wedding cake they'd been commissioned to bake for a local wedding. Lexy sighed, watching Cassie's pink-tipped, blonde, spiked hair bob up and down with her efforts. The two girls had been best friends since high school and Nans was like a second grandmother to Cassie. She was probably right—Nans *did* have quite an active social life.

Looking around the kitchen of *The Cup and Cake* from her spot in the doorway, Lexy felt a swell of pride. The stainless steel appliances gleamed, the floors and counters were scrubbed clean and the air was spiced with the sweet smell of baking. It was her dream come true, thanks to her parents. They had loaned her a large sum of money to open the bakery when they'd sold their home and bought an RV to fulfill *their* dream of traveling the country.

Lexy's swell of pride deflated into a gnawing of uneasiness as she remembered what Nans had said on the phone the night before. Her parents had been having trouble with the RV. They hadn't mentioned anything to her, but of course they wouldn't, because they wouldn't want her to worry. This made it even more important for her to get cracking on this case, so they could put Jack's house up for sale. Her parents had given her the ability to live out her dream and she didn't want *their* dream to suffer because they needed RV repairs. She had to pay them back right away, which meant she'd have to start investigating today, whether Nans wanted to help or not.

But first, she needed to try a variation of her meringue recipe. She glanced out at the front of the shop. The cafe tables set up next to the large window were all empty, giving her a clear view to the waterfall across the street. The morning coffee crowd was gone and the lunch-timers hadn't straggled in yet. She and Cassie usually used this time to bake, each girl taking turns to wait on any customers who wandered in.

Lexy caught a whiff of fresh-brewed coffee from the self-serve coffee stations as she turned her attention back to the kitchen. A pile of ingredients waited for her on the six-foot long butcher-block island that ran down the middle of the room.

The bells over the front door would alert them if a customer came in, so she made her way to the table and grabbed four eggs from the basket where she'd placed them hours ago so they could acclimate to room temperature.

"It's strange that Nans isn't jumping all over this. She must have heard about it through the grapevine by now, even if she didn't understand my call last night," Lexy said as she cracked the eggs, expertly separating the whites from the yolks. "Did John mention anything to you about it?"

Lexy often relied on Cassie to give her the scoop on various cases she was interested in because Jack was incredibly tight-lipped about police business. Luckily, Jack's partner, John Darling, wasn't as tight-lipped and, since he was married to Cassie, Lexy easily found out about the goings on down at the Brook Ridge Falls Police Department.

Cassie rolled her eyes. "He said Davies is acting like she found Jimmy Hoffa."

"Jeez, I hope she doesn't screw things up. She told Jack he was a suspect!"

"I know." Cassie stuck a tiny silver ball into the center of a flower on the cake. "John said that was just standard procedure. He's sure Jack will be cleared once they sift through the clues."

Lexy added salt, cream of tartar and a little vanilla extract to the egg whites, set the hand mixer inside the bowl and turned it on.

"Anyway, I'm stopping over at Nans after I get this new recipe in the oven. Will you watch the shop for me?" Lexy yelled over the sound of the beater.

"Of course." Cassie glanced up from her work. "So, tell me, what does a mummy look like, exactly, and how does a body get that way?"

"Brown and leathery ... I was surprised, but it really did look a lot like an old Egyptian mummy. I guess that's what happens when a body is sealed up with not a lot of air circulation."

"You'd think it would have smelled all this time."

"It probably did at first." Lexy turned off the beater and stuck a spoon into the egg white mixture, pulled it out slowly and watched the resulting peak carefully. It stood straight up. Perfect. She checked her recipe notes, which she'd adjusted to use a pinch more sugar than the ones she'd made the day before. She measured the sugar into a cup. "Jack said it would be long past smelling by now."

"It must have smelled at first, though ... you'd think the neighbors would have noticed."

Lexy poured a little of the sugar into the egg mixture and turned the beater on again. "Jack said he thought it might have been the builder that hid the body. I mean, I can't imagine the nice couple that lived in his house being involved. I think all those houses were built around the same time, so there were probably no neighbors to notice the smell."

"I guess that makes sense. It must have been scary finding that in the basement and then realizing it had been there the whole time. Was there anything else in there with the body?"

Lexy added a little more sugar and turned on the beater. "Just the clothes and the sachets."

"Sachets?"

"Yeah, you know those little perfumed pouches you put in your drawers? These still smelled like lavender. I guess they never lose their smell, even after being sealed up with a mummy."

"They were sealed up in there with it?"

"Yep. I assume the killer thought it would mask the smell."

"Really?" Cassie scrunched her face up. "What kind of builder carries around lavender sachets?"

Lexy added the rest of the sugar and beat it into the egg whites carefully, her mind trying to conjure up an image of a burly builder with lavender sachets in his pockets. She was pretty sure no builder would be caught dead with them.

Which begged the question—who the heck put them in there?

Chapter Four

Lexy finished with the meringues and loaded the batches she'd made earlier in the morning into two white boxes, which she secured with old-fashioned pink and white striped baker's twine. One box was for Nans and the other for her first stop—the previous owners of Jack's house, Charlie and Lois McDonald.

She pulled her VW Beetle onto Main Street, then followed that to County Road. The assisted living complex the McDonalds had moved to was several miles away, off County Road. The traffic was almost nonexistent and Lexy let herself relax while she drank in the blue skies, lush woods, and occasional cow-dotted field along the way.

She was almost at her destination when a blue car coming the other way jolted her out of her driving trance.

Was that Ruth's Oldsmobile?

She squinted out the windshield as the two cars drew closer to one another. It was the same blue color and make as Ruth's 1970s Olds and, as far as Lexy knew, Ruth was the only one in the county that drove one. It *had* to be her.

But something was odd. Ruth rarely drove the car and when she did it was usually to shuttle Nans, Ida and Helen somewhere in search of clues ... and *that* was only when they couldn't talk Lexy into driving them. But she didn't see the usual four heads sticking up—there was only one.

As the cars passed each other, her heart skipped a beat. The driver was Nans.

Lexy tooted the horn and waved, but Nans paid no mind. Her eyes stared straight ahead, her hands gripping the steering wheel at the ten o'clock and two o'clock positions. Lexy wasn't surprised that her grandmother was unwaveringly focused on driving. Nans hardly ever drove anymore, which made her wonder what was so important that Nans would strike out in the car by herself.

She didn't have long to ponder it, though, because the turnoff to the assisted living was upon her. She parked, grabbed her white bakery box and headed inside. Lexy had met the McDonalds several years ago through Nans. She knew that Charlie had some problems walking and they had moved to this facility as opposed to the Brook Ridge Retirement Center, where Nans lived, because this one offered private apartments with assistance on site, but she had no idea what unit they lived in.

Lexy had stopped in at the office and was directed to apartment 112 where she now stood, rapping on the door loudly.

The lock clicked and a vaguely familiar, wrinkled face peered out.

"Mrs. McDonald?"

The woman nodded.

"Do you remember me? I'm Mona Baker's granddaughter, Lexy." She held up the white box. "I brought you some meringue cookies."

"Why, Lexy. Yes, of course. Do come in." Lois opened the door wider and Lexy could see Charlie standing behind her. Neither of them seemed *that* surprised to see her, but Lexy figured at their age, not much was surprising.

The apartment was small, but neat as a pin. To the right was a kitchen with almond Formica cabinets and a matching Formica counter. Stainless steel appliances winked at her. The kitchen was open, with a breakfast bar opening to a small dining area.

"Good to see you, Lexy," Charlie let go of the grip on his walker and his strong handshake surprised Lexy. He motioned to the living room in front of them. "Come on in."

Charlie ushered her over to a beige leatherette sofa while Lois rushed the box into the kitchen.

"This is a lovely surprise, Lacey," Lois shot over her shoulder as she arranged the cookies on a pink Depression-era glass plate.

"Lexy."

"Yes, of course. Sorry Lucy." Lois plopped the plate of cookies on the coffee table and tapped her head. "The memory isn't what it used to be."

"How *is* Mona?" Charlie turned to Lois. "We haven't seen her in months, right dear?"

"That's right. I hope she is doing well." Lois turned to Lexy.

"Very well." *At least, I think she is.*

"Did you bake these?" Charlie pointed at the cookies.

"Yes. I own the bakery *The Cup and Cake* downtown. I'm trying out a new recipe for the Brook Ridge Falls annual dessert contest." Lexy picked up the plate and held it out to him. "Please, try one."

Charlie took a cookie and Lexy passed the plate over to Lois. Then they all sat there looking at each other.

Lexy decided to get down to business. "I don't know if you know this, but I married the man that bought your house."

"Oh?" Lois raised her brow. "That's nice, dear."

"Yes. Well, anyway, we were cleaning out the basement—"

"Such a nice young man he was, wasn't he, Mother?" Charlie interrupted.

"Oh, yes." Lois nodded. "I think he was a butcher."

"No, I believe he was a gardener."

Lois narrowed her eyes. "No, that's not it either. I'm pretty sure he was a food critic."

"No, dear. He was a—."

"He's a police detective." Lexy had to cut Charlie off or she feared they'd go on like this all day.

"Yes, that's right." Lois nodded and settled back in her chair. "Anyway, what did you say about the bathroom?"

"The basement."

"Oh, yes. That house had a nice, large one. Did he refinish it? We were always going to do that." Charlie's expression turned wistful.

"No. It was full. Of your stuff," Lexy said. "That's actually why I'm here."

Lois waved her hand around. "Oh, whatever you find down there you can keep, dear. Isn't that right, Charlie?"

"Yes, of course. As you can see, we don't have much room here."

"It's not about the items. I was wondering about the basement itself," Lexy said. "Did you ever notice anything strange about it?"

"The Grange Hall? No, I don't think we had anything down there from the Grange Hall." Lois bit into her meringue cookie and made a face.

"No, not the Grange—I said *strange*. Did you notice anything unusual about the basement ... a smell, or maybe something about the walls?"

Lois and Charlie looked at each other and shrugged.

"I think we had some beach balls and probably a few tennis balls," Charlie said. "Lois here used to be quite the tennis player in her day."

The two of them fell silent, reveling in their old memories, judging by the wistful smiles on their faces. Disappointment prickled through Lexy's veins. She hadn't gotten any useful information from the McDonalds.

Were they too senile to be reliable?

She didn't know what she was hoping to find out. If Jack's theory of the killer being the builder was true, then the McDonalds most likely had no idea what was hidden in their basement ... and Lexy certainly wasn't going to be the one to tell them. They'd find out soon enough.

"When you bought the house, did you notice the basement walls were strange?"

"Oh, we were so excited. It was our first house, you know. We were going to decorate the basement like a speakeasy ... we planned to finish the walls off and ..." Lois's voice trailed off and she shrugged. "We started to do a little remodeling down there, but then life got in the way and we just started using it as storage."

"We never really did a lot down there. It was just storage," Charlie added.

"Did you notice the builder acting strange or anything that seemed out of place right after you moved in? You were the first people to move in on that street, right?"

"Oh, no, Mona was there already, and Paddy and Mary Sullivan. Floyd Nichols had just moved in the week before us. The builder was very nice and it was a wonderful neighborhood. We were all very close back in the day," Charlie said.

"Yes," Lois added. "We had a lot of fun. Lots of backyard parties and barbecues. People just don't do that sort of thing anymore." Lois's eyes turned sad. "I guess they prefer to stay inside, watching cable TV or tweeting and posting on Facebook."

Lexy was taken aback. If people already lived in the neighborhood, wouldn't they have smelled something? Especially Nans, who lived right behind them. Lexy felt certain the neighbors would have had some sort of welcoming party if they were as close as Lois said.

"And none of your new neighbors mentioned anything odd about your house when you moved in?"

"Odd? No, not our house." Charlie pressed his lips together and looked at the ceiling. "There was this one incident years after we moved in. Apparently, a stranger was seen skulking around the neighborhood."

Lexy's ears perked up. "A stranger? What do you mean?"

Lois shrugged. "I'm not sure. We just heard about it when we got back ... we were on vacation in Europe that summer but there was definitely a suspicious stranger around." She glanced at Charlie. "Right?"

"That's right. They told us about it when we got back. Someone with a tattered sweatshirt who didn't fit in. The neighbors were in an uproar."

"I was a little nervous because they claimed he was near our house. But that was so long ago I barely remember." Lois stood and helped Charlie out of his chair, then they made their way toward the door.

Lexy didn't want to overstay her welcome, but she figured she could get one last question in. "When you came back from vacation, did you notice anything strange about the house?"

Lois and Charlie glanced at each other. "No, dear, we didn't have any problems with mice ... did you say you saw a mouse?"

"No. No mouse." Lexy slipped through the door Lois was now holding open, then turned back to look at the couple. "Well, it was nice talking to you."

"You, too, dear, and thank you for the cookies." Lois leaned toward her, her voice lowered to a whisper. "They were very good, but they could use a touch more sugar."

Chapter Five

Lexy wasn't surprised she didn't get anything useful from the McDonalds. If Jack's theory about the builder was true, they wouldn't know anything about how the body got in their basement. Although the information about the stranger certainly was interesting—she'd have to ask Nans about that. But Lois and Charlie had said the stranger was seen years after they'd bought the house, so it probably wasn't related. And besides, Lexy didn't know how much she could trust what they said—they seemed rather confused about a lot of things.

Nans still hadn't called her back, but Lexy needed to continue on without her. Jack had said the first thing to do was find out more about the builder, but how did one find out information on someone who built a house over sixty years ago, and was probably retired or dead by now? Lexy figured the best way was to use the internet, and if anyone could dig up the info it would be Nans' friends—two of the members of the *Ladies Detective Club*—Ruth and Helen.

And that's exactly where she was headed, to the Brook Ridge Retirement Center where she could, hopefully, catch up with Nans and fill the four ladies in on the grave discovery in Jack's basement.

Gray clouds had rolled in, spoiling the blue sky and causing a light sprinkle as Lexy pulled into the retirement community parking lot. She grabbed her box of meringues and sprinted for the glass door that

40

opened into the lobby, holding the box over her head as a makeshift umbrella.

The door whooshed shut behind her and she turned left to go down the hallway to Nans apartment.

"Yoo-hoo! Lexy, is that you?" Ida's voice rang out from behind her and Lexy turned to see Ruth, Helen, and Ida sitting at one of the round tables in the spacious lobby that doubled as a gathering room.

"Hi!" Lexy changed direction and headed toward them, frowning at the empty fourth seat where Nans would normally be sitting.

"She's not here." Ruth stated the obvious.

"I thought I saw her driving your car earlier," Lexy said.

Ruth nodded. "Yep. She asked to borrow it. Mighty odd, if you ask me."

Ida and Helen nodded in agreement.

"I think she's up to something," Ida whispered.

"Maybe she's out visiting that nice young man from the square dance," Ruth offered.

Lexy's brows flew up. "Young man?"

"Oh, of course *you* wouldn't think he was young, but there was a gentleman at the square dance who seemed quite taken with your grandmother and I swear he couldn't have been a day over seventy-five." Helen turned to Ruth and Ida. "Don't you think, girls?"

"Oh, yeah. She's a cougar," Ida said.

Lexy scrunched up her face. She'd never considered that Nans might someday have a boyfriend. Her grandmother hadn't seemed interested in any men since her grandfather had died. But, now that Lexy thought about it, a male friend might be good for Nans. She wanted her grandmother to be happy and felt relieved that her strange behavior could be attributed to a man and not something more serious.

"Oh, thank goodness. I was afraid something was wrong with her," Lexy said. "Did she say when she'd be back?"

"Nope." Ida raised a brow at the box. "What have you got there?"

Lexy set the box on the table, untied the string and flipped open the lid. Ida craned her neck to peer inside.

"Meringue cookies?"

"Yes, but I didn't bring any plates or napkins," Lexy said.

"Oh, no worries." Ida pulled her giant beige patent leather purse from the back of her chair, rummaged inside for a few seconds, then pulled out a stack of napkins and passed them around.

Lexy slipped into the empty seat as the ladies gingerly picked cookies out of the box and set them on their respective napkins. She'd baked three different kinds—a rich, brown coffee flavor, an orange and white striped that had a slight orange tang, and her favorite, a plain vanilla meringue that was piped over a chocolate kiss so that the kiss acted as a surprise chocolate center.

"I'm trying to find the perfect recipe to enter in the Brook Ridge Falls annual dessert contest. Maybe you guys can help me decide which one to use." Lexy smiled at the ladies, but her smile faded when she noticed them staring at her, wide-eyed, instead of attacking the cookies with their usual gusto. "What's wrong?"

"Did you say you were entering the annual dessert contest?" Ida asked.

"Yeah. It's the first time I've entered and I'm very excited about it." Lexy wondered why the ladies did not seem to be sharing her enthusiasm—they were usually quite supportive of her.

"Oh, you might want to rethink that," Ruth said.

"What? Why?"

"Because you'll be going up against Violet Switzer," Helen answered.

"Who?"

"Maybe you haven't heard of her, but we have and she's not one to be trifled with." Ida shook her head.

Lexy's brow wrinkled. "What do you mean?"

"She's ruthless and cunning. She'll do anything to win a contest. Some say she'd just as soon kill you as give up the blue ribbon." Helen thrust her chin out at Ida. "Just ask Ida."

Lexy raised a brow at Ida.

Ida nodded. "Yep. I went up against her in the Old Home Day pea-shooting contest back in fifty-five ... or was it fifty-six? Well, whatever year it was, she was mean as a stuck toad and I'm sure the passing decades haven't made her any nicer."

"Pea-shooting?" Lexy stared at Ida.

"Yeah. You know, you take a hollow tube and put a pea in, then blow. I used to be the champion shooter. Won every contest for decades." Ida's chin tilted up proudly. "I have very good lungs."

"But then Violet showed up and blew Ida out of the water. No pun intended." Helen giggled.

Ida sighed. "She sure can shoot far, but it was the way she went about it. Following me and sizing me up. Then she would try to intimidate me into bowing out." Ida pressed her lips together. "But I do have to admit she won fair and square. 'Course they don't have that contest anymore."

"Right, I think they replaced that with the cherry pit spitting contest," Ruth said.

"She wins that one, too."

"And she bakes, too?" Lexy asked.

"Bakes, gardens, knits." Ida picked a cookie up from her napkin. "You name it and Violet is into it."

"Well, I'm not afraid of some old lady that can shoot a pea through a straw," Lexy said.

"No? You just wait. Anyway, we know that's not the main reason you came." Ruth leaned toward her and lowered her voice. "Our informant down at BRFPD told us about the mummy and we figured you'd be coming by."

"Been sitting here waiting on 'ya," Ida added.

"Oh, good," Lexy said. "I called Nans last night first thing, but I guess we had a bad connection. I'm surprised she's not here waiting, too. I'm sure she must have heard about the mummy by now."

"Yeah, her new boyfriend must be more interesting," Ida cackled.

"We can get started without her," Helen said. "Tell us what you know."

Lexy glanced around the room. The other tables were empty, but two gray-haired men sat in the lounge chairs, watching the big screen TV that was turned up to an annoyingly high volume.

"Oh, don't mind them." Helen waved her hand toward the two men. "They're deaf as doornails. Won't hear a word we're saying."

Lexy told the ladies about how they'd found the mummy and Jack's theory about the builder. Then she went on to describe her visit earlier with the McDonalds. "And, of course, Davies said that Jack is a suspect."

"Oh, dear! That's crazy," Helen said as she bit into the chocolate kiss meringue.

"Well, a dead body *was* found in his basement."

"But surely they can tell it was put there before he moved in ... I mean, that must have been what happened, right?" Ruth asked.

"If Jack is a suspect, that's all the more reason for *The Ladies' Detective Club* to investigate and help clear his name," Ida said.

That's right." Ruth pressed her lips together and tapped them with her index finger. "Are you sure the previous owners weren't hiding something from you? If they're the killers, they might be very clever."

"They're just a nice old couple," Lexy said. "It couldn't be them. Plus, they didn't seem to have a clue of what I was talking about. And anyway, Jack said he figured it would be the builder since he would have had a perfect opportunity to make that secret room and hide the body when he was building the house."

Ida frowned down at her half-eaten meringue cookie. "Wouldn't the smell of a decaying body hamper the sale?"

Lexy shrugged. "I guess he might have stalled the sale until that smell was gone."

"What about the other people coming on the job site?" Ruth asked. "Or the neighbors. Surely, someone would notice something."

"Wait a minute," Helen said. "We're talking about Jack's house, and that's right behind Mona's. Did she live there then or did she buy the house after the McDonalds?"

"The McDonalds said that she already lived there when they moved in," Lexy offered.

"Nothing gets past Mona, so if she lived there back then, she must have noticed something." Ida's forehead creased and she craned her neck to look in the parking lot. "Where *is* she, anyway?"

Lexy turned to follow her gaze, but there was no sign of Ruth's big, blue Oldsmobile. "Beats me."

"Did the McDonalds tell you who the builder was?" Helen pulled Lexy's attention from the window.

"No. I guess I should have asked."

"No worries." Ruth bent down and picked up a giant black purse from under her chair. She opened a flap, unzipped a compartment, reached in and pulled out an iPad. "Google is a wonderful tool. We'll just look it up."

"It would help to know who the victim was, too." Helen raised her brows at Lexy. "Any idea?"

"No. Sorry."

"Could you tell if it was a man or woman?"

"I think it was a man," Lexy said. "It was wearing shorts and what looked like a tank top or white undershirt. That's not something a woman usually wears."

"Very good." Ida nodded at Lexy. "And that's an important clue."

"It is?"

"Yes. From the clothing, we know it must have been summer when he was killed."

"So, now we just need to look for missing persons reports on males that disappeared in the summer." Helen reached into her giant purse and produced an iPad. "Now, what year was the house built?"

"I'm not sure exactly." Lexy chewed her bottom lip. "Jack said about sixty years ago."

"Okay, good enough."

Ruth and Helen alternated tapping away on their iPads and nibbling the meringue cookies. Ida looked over Ruth's shoulder while nibbling her own cookie. Lexy noticed that they weren't eating the cookies with their usual gusto. She hoped that was simply because their minds were too busy with investigating to pay much attention to the cookies, and not because the cookies didn't taste good.

"That's strange," Helen said. "I've searched several decades and not found anyone reported missing who was never found."

"Maybe he wasn't from around here," Ida suggested.

"Maybe. But it seems like he would be. Otherwise, why did he get killed and hidden here?" Ida asked. "It doesn't seem like one would bring a body from somewhere else and seal it up in a basement, does it?"

"Well, we can just ask the builder, because I've found him," Ruth announced.

"Really?" Ida craned her neck to look at Ruth's iPad. "Was he involved in any nefarious activity? Money laundering? Fraud? Murder?"

"No. Nothing."

"Is he even still alive?" Lexy asked.

"Oh, yes. In fact, he lives right here."

Ida wrinkled her brow. "In the retirement center?"

"Yep. Tommy O'Keefe, 350 Pinewood."

"Oh? He has one of the single homes. Those are expensive, so he must have money." Ida's blue eyes danced with excitement. "Probably got it by being paid off to hide bodies in the homes he built."

Helen swatted Ida's arm. "Oh, Ida, you do have an imagination!"

"I think we need to make a visit to him, ladies. What do you think?" Ida asked.

"Definitely," Helen answered.

They all looked at Ruth for her answer but she was squinting intently at something past Lexy's shoulder, apparently not having heard them.

"Isn't that Mona?" Ruth asked.

Lexy spun in the direction of Ruth's gaze. "Yes, she must not see us."

"Mona! Yoo-hoo. We're over here!" Ida yelled.

Nans stopped short, then slowly turned toward them. Lexy thought she saw a look of uncertainty cross her grandmother's face, but then she broke into a smile and headed toward them.

"Where have you been?" Ida asked.

Nans face flushed and she looked down at the floor. "Oh, you know, just some errands. What are you all doing?"

"We're discussing our new case," Helen said.

"New case?"

"Yes," Ida nodded enthusiastically. "The basement mummy case. You know, the one Lexy found in Jack's basement."

"Oh, right." Nans waved her hand. "I heard about that. Very unusual."

"I'll say!" Ruth pulled a chair over from the next table and indicated for Nans to sit. "So, anyway, tell us what *you* know and we'll fill you in on what we've found out."

"Know? Why would I know anything?" Nans asked.

"You lived there back then. Surely, you've thought back and remembered something that might have been amiss," Helen prompted.

"We don't even know *when* it happened." Nans turned to Lexy. "Do we?"

"Not really. I mean, the police haven't said anything, but Jack thinks it happened when the house was being built."

Nans raised a brow. "Oh, really? So they can't pinpoint the time of death?"

"I'm not sure." Lexy looked around the table at the other ladies. "Can they pinpoint the time of death with a body that's been mummified?"

The three ladies shrugged.

"You lived there before they built the house, right, Mona?" Ruth asked.

Nans nodded. "So whenever it happened, you *were* living there. You must have seen something," Helen said. "Think back. Did you notice any strange activity at night? An odd smell? If you want, I can hypnotize you to help you remember."

"Certainly not!" Nans said. "I mean, I don't need any *help* remembering. My memory is just fine and I tell you, I never saw anything strange going on."

"Well, we've found the builder and he lives right here in the complex. We intend to pay him a visit. Maybe you could bake one of your apple pies," Helen suggested. Nans' apple pies were famous, and the ladies had discovered long ago that bringing pies or pastry to interrogate ...err ... visit ... a suspect was a great way to get them to open up.

"Oh, I don't know." Nans grimaced. "I have a pretty full schedule."

"You don't know?" Ida gave Nans an incredulous look. "Jack is a suspect and that Watson Davies character could screw things up for him. We *have* to investigate, for Jack's sake."

"Davies might be a little hard to get along with, but she does a fine job," Nans said. "Remember how she uncovered the killer when we had that whole fiasco with your wedding dress, Lexy?"

"Sure, but I think we helped her on that one. And on the copycat baker case, too."

Nans tsked. "Maybe, but she's perfectly capable of figuring out this old case. Anyway, it happened so long ago, who would even care about it now?"

Lexy squinted at Nans. "I would think you would care."

"Yeah, aren't you going to investigate with us?" Ruth asked.

Nans shrugged. "I need to look over the new cases. Maybe if there's nothing else more interesting. I'm very busy and have to pick my cases carefully. You know, some things from the past are better left in the past."

Lexy exchanged a glance with Ruth, Ida and Helen.

Since when did Nans not want to investigate every case?

"But for now, I need to get upstairs. I have some calls to make." Nans slid the keys across the table to Ruth. "Thanks for the loaner."

Nans stood, plucked a meringue cookie from the box and took a bite. She turned to leave, swallowed then looked down at Lexy. "This is good, but it needs a bit more sugar."

And with that, Nans shuffled off across the lobby, leaving Lexy, Ruth, Ida and Helen staring after her.

Chapter Six

"Do these seem like they need more sugar to you?" Lexy held one of the orange and vanilla meringue cookies out to Cassie.

Lexy had been a bit concerned the day before with Ruth, Ida and Helen's unusual silence about the cookies. The three ladies usually raved about Lexy's baking, so she figured that was their way of politely telling her they didn't like the taste. Nans had said they needed more sugar, which Lexy found hard to believe since she'd upped the amount for that recipe, but she took the advice and had come to the bakery early to bake another batch with a teaspoon more sugar.

That batch was now cooling in the oven, but she wanted Cassie's opinion on the recipe from the day before just to be sure she was doing the right thing.

Cassie bit into the cookie. She scrunched up her face comically, then swished the bite around in her mouth. She swallowed, then nodded. "Yep. Just a tad, though."

"Thanks. Maybe today's batch is sweeter." Lexy glanced over at the oven. She'd turned it off an hour ago and resisted the urge to peek in. The secret to perfect meringues was letting them cool slowly, and opening the oven would let in a rush of cold air, so she willed herself to be patient until the timer went off.

The smell of almonds drifted over from the counter, where Cassie was drizzling icing on a batch of almond scones. Lexy's mouth watered as she sidled over to the tray, reaching her hand out for one of the freshly drizzled pieces.

"I think I need to taste test this," Lexy said. "I rushed in here early to bake these meringues for my visit to the builder of Jack's house and I'm starving."

Cassie raised a pierced brow as Lexy took a bite. "You found the builder?"

"Yep. Ruth found him on the internet." Lexy broke off a corner of the scone while she finished chewing the piece she had in her mouth. "Did you hear anything more about the case from John? Davies won't tell Jack a thing, and last night Jack said he hadn't had a chance to catch up with anyone else in the department about it."

"No. He said Davies was doing all kinds of tests to figure out who the mummy was—when he died, and what killed him."

"Do you think they can pinpoint any of those things?"

Cassie shrugged. "Who knows? Jack must be anxious, though."

"He's trying to act like he's not, but I think he is." Lexy's heart twisted as she remembered their good-bye kiss earlier that morning. Jack had asked her to check in with him right after they talked to the builder and she could tell he was nervous. "But I think he'll be cleared soon since he's helping us on the case."

"That must be a rare treat for Nans and the ladies —usually it's *them* helping *him*."

Ding!

The timer announced that the meringues were ready and Lexy shoved the rest of the scone in her mouth, her taste buds delighting in the sweet icing and cake-like scone. She crunched one of the slivered almonds that had been sprinkled on top as she slowly opened the oven door.

She held her breath and peered inside, relieved to see rows of perfectly puffed meringue cookies, their tops peaking in a swirl. Perfect. She slid the tray out of the oven and grabbed a white bakery box, then carefully placed the cookies in the box.

Lexy untied her apron and pulled it over her head, smoothing her white, sleeveless blouse and checking her tan capris for spots of flour. Satisfied with her appearance, she grabbed the box and headed toward the door.

"I'm off to meet the ladies and visit Mr. O'Keefe," she called to Cassie.

"Okay, I'll hold down the fort," Cassie said. "Good luck."

Fifteen minutes later, Lexy pulled up in front of the retirement center, where the ladies were waiting anxiously at the door. They descended on her VW Beetle like a swarm of ants to a picnic and somehow Ruth, Ida and Helen managed to fold themselves into the tiny backseat while Nans slid into the passenger seat. Lexy always marveled at the dexterity the ladies displayed when getting into her car—they claimed it was all due to practicing yoga.

Helen poked her head in between the two front seats. "Thanks for picking us up, Lexy."

"You're welcome."

"O'Keefe's house is only about a half-mile up the hill, but we don't want to walk in our good shoes," Ida added.

"Plus, Ida's bunion is acting up," Ruth said and they all chuckled, except Ida, who elbowed Ruth in the ribs.

"I'm glad you decided to join us today," Lexy said to Nans as she drove across the parking lot to the road that led to the retirement center's single family homes.

"Well, I guess if you guys are going to investigate, I'll tag along." Nans half turned so that she could address everyone. "I'm just not sure this case warrants our time. And anyway, it seems cut and dried that it's the builder. But if the police can't pinpoint the time of death, then how can they prove it?"

"I'm not sure about that," Lexy said. "Cassie told me that Davies was running some tests to figure out when he died."

Nans swiveled her head toward Lexy. "Did she say how accurate they can be?"

"No."

"If its within days then that can help, but if its within years, I don't see how that would be of much use."

"Here's the house right here." Ruth shoved her hand in-between the front seats, her index finger pointing at a large, Tudor-style house on the right.

Lexy pulled into the driveway, eyeing the carpet of green grass and perfectly manicured shrubs that were ringed by purple, red and white flowers. It sure did look like Mr. O'Keefe had money, just like Ida had said. The question was ... did he get that money from building homes or from something else?

"I don't think we'll find out much here." Nans stepped out of the car and folded the front seat over for Ida, Ruth and Helen.

"Why not?" Helen asked. "If he's the killer, I'm sure he'll slip up somehow."

"That's right." Ruth started up the walkway. "Besides, we have a sixth sense for these things. If he's guilty, we'll know."

They reached the polished oak door and everyone looked toward Nans to take the lead as she usually did. Nans, however, didn't seem to want to take the lead and got busy studying her nails, so Ida pushed her way to the front of the group and punched the doorbell. "You guys let me do the talking. Just follow my lead."

The doorbell chimed and, after a few seconds, the door opened to reveal a pleasant-looking, white-haired gentleman who raised bushy white brows at them. His lips curled in a welcoming smile.

"Well, what can I do for you ladies?"

Ida glanced back at them and Lexy knew what she was thinking—he was acting awfully nice for a cold-blooded killer.

"We're neighbors from the retirement center," Ida said. "We've come on a welcoming visit."

His brows knit together in confusion. "Really? I've been living here for quite some time."

"Oh, we know. It takes us a while to get to everyone." Ida grabbed the bakery box from Lexy and held it up. "We brought cookies from *The Cup and Cake* downtown. Lexy here is the owner."

"Oh. Well, if there are cookies, then please come in." He pushed the door wide and they all filed into an oak-floored foyer.

"I'm Ida and this is Ruth, Helen, Lexy and Mona." Ida held her hand out.

"Tom O'Keefe." Tom favored each of them with a firm handshake, then turned down the hall. "Come on in to the kitchen."

Lexy peeked into the rooms as they followed him down the hall. The furnishings were expensive, but tasteful. Not opulent. The rooms were clean. The large kitchen at the back of the house boasted a panoramic view from the top of the hill along with stainless steel appliances, granite counters and an impressive fieldstone fireplace. Tom set the box down on the oversized kitchen island and bent down to rummage in the cabinet.

"How long have you ladies lived here?" His muffled voice came from inside the cabinet. "I don't believe I've met any of you."

"Ruth's been here for about ten years now. I've been here for seven and Helen and Mona have only lived here for a few years," Ida said. "Lexy is Mona's granddaughter. She doesn't live here, of course."

Tom surfaced from the cabinet and put a round platter on the island.

"I see she's got a few years before she's of age," he said, winking at Lexy as he took the cookies from the box and put them on the platter.

"Those are made from a new recipe Lexy is fixing to enter in the Brook Ridge Dessert contest," Ruth said.

"You don't say. Well, I feel honored to be trying them." Tom gestured toward the long, pine table and the ladies sat while Tom pulled some smaller plates out of one of the upper cabinets.

"Would you like some tea?" he asked.

"That would be lovely, wouldn't it girls?" Ida raised her brows at Lexy and the ladies, and they all murmured their agreement while Tom filled a kettle with water and got busy passing out dainty tea cups and saucers.

"So, we heard you were a builder here in town," Ida ventured, once they were all settled with steaming cups of tea and cookies on their plates.

Tom paused the cookie halfway to his lips. "Yes, I built many of the houses here in town. But that was years ago. I'm retired now."

"That must have been quite lucrative," Ruth chimed in, looking pointedly around the well-equipped kitchen.

Tom narrowed amused eyes at Ruth. "Why, yes it was."

Ida fixed him with a hawk-like stare. "Not all builders make out this good. Most of the ones I know are flat broke."

"Well, I invested my money wisely." Tom aimed a dazzling smile at Ida. "I'm not sure why the interest. Are you ladies trying to fix me up with someone?"

"That could be a possibility," Ida said. "Really, we're just interested in our neighbors, right girls?"

The others nodded and Lexy noticed Nans had been paying more attention to the crumbs on her plate than the conversation. What was up with her? Lexy wondered if Nans really did have a boyfriend. She was certainly acting distracted enough.

Lexy's eyes strayed past Nans to the pine mantle on the fieldstone fireplace, where a row of trophies was displayed.

"Those are my dart contest trophies," Tom said proudly. "I haven't played in years, but I used to be quite good."

"It looks like you won a lot," Lexy agreed.

"Oh, yes. I was the dart champion ten years in a row down at *The Elms Pub*." Tom gestured toward the trophies. "I would have been champion ten more years, too, if it wasn't for *her*."

Helen's brows shot up. "Her?"

Tom's mouth twisted in a grimace. "I know I shouldn't hold a grudge. It's silly, really, and that was so long ago, but *that woman* took competition to a whole new level."

Ida sucked in a loud breath. "I think I know *exactly* who you are talking about."

Tom turned to look at Ida and they both said it at the same time.

"Violet Switzer."

"You know her?" Tom asked.

Ida nodded. "I used to be the pea-shooting champ until she came to town."

Tom laughed. "Well, I guess I feel a little better that I'm not the only one she targeted."

"Oh, she was nasty," Ida said. "Did she stalk you and try to intimidate you?"

"Yes." Tom's face flushed. "I'm embarrassed to admit it, but her tactics worked."

Lexy felt seeds of doubt sprout in her stomach. This Violet person sounded downright nasty and now Lexy was going up against her. She glanced at the plates on the table. No one had even finished one cookie! Maybe entering the dessert contest wasn't such a good idea, after all.

"So, if you hung out at *The Elms Pub*, you probably built a lot of houses over in the Elms section of town," Ruth said, pulling Lexy from her thoughts.

"Oh, yeah, I built most of those homes," Tom said proudly.

"Then you must have built Mona's." Ida nodded her head toward Nans, who looked up from swishing her tea bag around in her cup.

"Yes, of course." Tom studied Nans. "I thought you looked familiar."

"Oh, I'm surprised you would remember after all these years," Nans said.

"I never forget a pretty face."

Nans blushed. Lexy, Ruth, Ida and Helen stared at her. It wasn't like her just to blush and not say anything.

Ida broke the silence. "You built the house behind her, too. You must have seen it on the news."

Tom looked at her curiously. "No, I don't watch the news. It's too depressing. What happened?"

"A secret room was discovered in their basement with a mummy in it."

Tom's brows slanted into a bushy 'V'. "Mummy? Like those things wrapped in gauze and buried with treasure?"

Ida nodded. "Yeah, except this one wasn't wrapped or buried with treasure."

"Someone had been murdered and placed inside the secret room," Ruth explained. "The body mummified due to the dry conditions and lack of air in the sealed room."

Tom looked shocked, and Lexy had to wonder if the look was about a mummy being in the basement or about the fact that the mummy had been discovered and now an investigation could lead police to the killer. "I never heard of that."

"Yep. It happens." Ida took a sip of tea, then said matter-of-factly. "So, since you built the house, you must have built that secret room."

Tom's head jerked back as if he'd been slapped. "What? I didn't put any secret room in any of my houses."

"But you must have. How else would it get there?"

"I assume the homeowner would have put it there. I have no idea what people do after I sell them." He rubbed his chin. "Just how did they discover this room, anyway?"

"My dog dug away the cement," Lexy said.

"*Your* dog? What was your dog doing there?"

"It's actually my husband's house now. We were cleaning out the basement to put it up for sale when my dog started barking and going crazy. I guess she must have sensed what was in there."

Tom narrowed his eyes. "So you demolished the wall because your dog barked?"

"Oh, no. She was digging at the cement and she dug out a hole. We looked in and discovered the mummy."

"Dug it out?" Tom shook his head. "That doesn't make any sense. I made the foundations out of cinderblock back then. Your dog couldn't dig a hole in that."

"No, of course not. This basement had a false wall that was wood-framed construction and she dug through some sort of cement-like coating that was on top of that."

Tommy's brows shot up. "Oh, right. *Now* I remember. A lot of people did that back then when they wanted to finish off the basement. They didn't like the look of the cinderblocks so they skimmed over it with a plaster-like compound that looked more appealing and helped waterproof and strengthen the walls."

Ida turned to Lexy. "So the wall matched the others because they all had the coating?"

"Yes."

"Well, that explains it. They probably just framed off the small section and plastered over it to make this secret room ... but who would do that?" Ida asked.

"I don't know, but I do know one thing." Ruth pointed her half-eaten cookie at them. "Whoever did it must have known they were going to put the body in there. Why else would they make a narrow room like that?"

"And that means it was premeditated murder," Helen added.

"The only people that would have had access at that point would have been the homeowners," Ida pointed out.

"I remember the McDonalds telling me they were going to have the basement refinished." Lexy still couldn't believe that nice, old couple would have been involved. "Maybe it was the guy who was going to refinish it."

"I seem to recall there was a guy who specialized in doing those restorations." Tom pressed his lips together and looked up while he searched his memory. "Was it Donny? No ... Bobby. Yes! His name was Bobby Nesbaum."

Ida glanced sharply at Nans. "Mona, do you remember anything about these basement renovations? You must have known about them. Did you have yours redone?"

"No. I didn't have mine done." Nans scrunched up her face. "I do seem to recall Lois and Charlie McDonald talking about it, but I don't know much. I think that person died, though, so it's probably no use trying to track him down."

Ida stared at Nans, then gave Lexy a funny look. It sure wasn't like Nans not to try to track down every clue and she'd seemed preoccupied the whole time. Worry started to nag at Lexy again. What if something was wrong with Nans? She shook off the worry. Nans was probably just having an off day or, like Ruth had suggested, she might have a new boyfriend that was occupying all her thoughts.

Tom started collecting the teacups, saving Lexy from having to think unwanted thoughts about her grandmother having a boyfriend, and they all stood to say their goodbyes.

As Tom walked them to the door, Lexy glanced at the expensive decor. Ida had made a good point earlier—she knew lots of builders and very few of them ended up with this kind of money. She made a mental note to check into Tom O'Keefe's background and finances.

Sure, he seemed sincere enough, but she'd learned that killers could seem that way when they were trying to cover their tracks. One thing was for sure. *Somebody* had made that room in the basement and only a couple of people would have had access. One of them was Tom and the other was the man Tom had eagerly (maybe too eagerly?) given them the name of—Bobby Nesbaum.

Chapter Seven

"So, how did your visit with the builder go? Do you think he's the killer?" Jack lifted up a corner of the shade in the kitchen window with his index finger and peered warily at the crime scene tape fluttering across the way in his backyard.

"I couldn't tell," Lexy answered. "He seemed surprised when we told him about finding the mummy and he did claim that he didn't finish the basements like that. He said he left them as cinder-block."

Jack let the shade drop and went back to washing the dishes. "Of course he would say that if he was trying to cover it up."

"I know. He didn't act suspicious at all. He's obviously not going to break down and confess, so how do we find out for sure?" Lexy picked up the plate Jack had placed in the strainer, wiped it dry, and put it away.

"We need to figure out the motive."

"And how do we do that?"

"Well, there're two main reasons people kill each other—money and passion. So we could look through his bank accounts and find out if he got a lot of money in. That might tell us if he was paid to hide the body. Of course, he could have killed him because he was being blackmailed, in which case we'd see a lot of money going out. I hope Davies is checking on these."

"I can have Ruth and Helen look, too. They seem to have access to things the rest of us don't have."

Jack chuckled. "Yeah, I've noticed. Usually, it annoys me when they hack into financial sites, but seeing as I can't use police resources myself, I guess I won't complain this time."

"So that takes care of the money. What about the passion?" Lexy stuffed the dishtowel inside the wine glass Jack had just washed out and rubbed it dry.

"For that, we need to find out if he had any enemies. If he was seen fighting with anyone or had a falling out." Jack shut off the water and looked at her. "Didn't Nans already suggest all this?"

Lexy sighed as she stood on her tiptoes to put the wine glass away. "Nans isn't herself and I'm a bit worried."

"How so?"

"She's acting disinterested in the case. She hardly even talked when we were at O'Keefe's and she's barely contributing any ideas. Ruth seems to think she has a boyfriend."

The corners of Jack's lips quirked up. "Boyfriend?"

"Yeah, some guy they met at the square dance. They said he was quite taken with her and then the next day, she borrowed Ruth's car and they think she went to see him!"

"Nans drove?"

"Yes, isn't that odd?" Lexy bent down to pet Sprinkles who had been watching them intently, just in case one of them dropped a morsel of food.

"And she's been acting preoccupied?"

Lexy looked up at Jack and nodded, a spasm of worry rippling through her heart.

Jack chuckled, pulled her to a standing position and folded her into his arms.

"You're silly. It's probably just the flush of first love." He looked into her eyes and said softly, ""Don't tell me you've forgotten how it is."

Lexy flushed. "No, I haven't."

"Right, so then give Nans a break. If she found someone, we should be glad for her. She deserves to be just as happy as we are, don't you think?"

"Yes." Lexy felt relieved. Jack was right, she was reading too much into this whole thing because she was so used to having Nans' full attention. If Nans had found herself a boyfriend, then Lexy would just have to learn to share her grandmother's time with him. She just hoped Nans would still want to investigate murders after the newness of her relationship wore off.

"And since you have me to guide you, I think we can handle this case without Nans, right?" Jack said.

"Right. So Ruth and Helen can handle looking into the finances, but how do we figure out if he had an enemy?""

Jack went back to the sink and turned on the water to wash the last of the dishes. "He's about Nans' age—did any of them know him?"

"No. Nans only knew him from buying the house and the other ladies weren't around here back then."

"Usually, we like to talk to someone who knew the suspect back then, a friend or relative—"

"Wait a minute! I think I know just where to ask," Lexy said, remembering the trophies from the pub. "And he did fight with someone, but she's very much alive."

"Who is that?" Jack rinsed off the last bowl and handed it to her.

"Violet Switzer."

"Who?"

Lexy told him about Violet, how she took competing to the extreme and had beaten Tom and Ida and was now Lexy's competition for the desserts contest. "I don't mind admitting that I'm a little intimidated by her already and I haven't even met her yet."

Jack laughed. "Well, she sounds intimidating, but I don't think Tom's grudge against her can be a clue since he didn't kill her."

"No, not her, but Sprinkles found that stub from *The Elms Pub* in your basement. What if that stub *was* from the mummy? Tom hung around there, too."

Jack pressed his lips together. "I don't think it was. Davies would never let a dog run off with a clue from the crime scene. I'm sure Sprinkles got that from somewhere else in the basement. But if Tom hung around there, then it is worth asking around to see if anyone who is still there knew him back then."

Lexy draped the dishtowel over the oven handle. "And I should go back to talk to the McDonalds again. They said they were *thinking* about redoing the basement but never actually had it done, so maybe they can verify the basement had that cement coating on the inside when they bought it."

"Now you're thinking!" Jack let the water out of the sink. "If they can verify that, it would prove O'Keefe was lying and had something to cover up."

Lexy felt a tingle of enthusiasm. Now she was getting somewhere. "Have you been able to get any information out of Davies?"

Jack shook his head. He lifted the corner of the shade with his index finger and looked back out the window. "No, she's clammed up tight. John's been feeding me whatever he can find out but she's not telling him much, either. All I know is that she's considering me as a suspect, but she can't do anything officially until she gets some more solid information. That's why it's so important we find out who did this right away."

Lexy's heart pinched at the worry on Jack's face. It wasn't doing him any good to stare out at the crime scene—she'd better do something to take his mind off it. She grabbed his arm and urged him away from the window.

"Don't worry, we'll sort this out," she said as she pulled him into the living room.

Jack plopped into a chair and pulled her into his lap. "You're right. I'm not all that worried."

He lowered his lips to Lexy's and her stomach did a little flip, but then a flash of light outside caught her eye. She turned her head toward the window, causing Jack's lips to brush her cheek.

Was someone out there watching them?"

She scrambled out of Jack's lap and ran to the window. Across the street sat a bright, red Mustang convertible with a white-haired old lady behind the wheel. And she wasn't just parked there—she was looking in Lexy's window with binoculars!

Lexy ripped the door open and ran out, but she was too late. The car screeched around the corner.

She closed the door and turned to Jack who was still sitting on the chair, his left brow raised at her.

"What was that all about?" he asked.

"Someone was outside looking in here with binoculars. I think they were stalking me!" Lexy fumed.

"Stalking you? Who would want to do that?"

"I'm not sure ... but I think it was Violet Switzer."

Chapter Eight

Lexy kept her eye on the rear-view mirror, looking for a red Mustang, as she drove to Nans' apartment the next morning. Pulling into the parking lot, she felt silly. Surely, Violet wouldn't follow her everywhere, and even if she did, what did Lexy care? She wasn't afraid of an old lady.

Her phone chirped and she looked down. Her mother. Lexy debated not answering because she was in a hurry to meet with Nans and the ladies, but guilt took over and she pressed the green button.

"Hi, Mom!"

"Lexy? Is that you?" Vera Baker's voice blasted out of the phone at its usual high volume, causing Lexy to hold the phone six inches away from her ear.

"Yes, Mom. How are you?"

"Oh, good, dear. What about you? Is Jack treating you okay?"

"Yes, he is, Mom. Where are you guys now?" Lexy had given up on trying to keep track of her nomadic parents who were traveling across North America in a haphazard manner. One week, they could be in Nevada, then the next week, Florida, then the next, Canada. There seemed to be no rhyme or reason to it, but Lexy figured if they were having a good time then who was she to question it?

"We're in the desert of Maine."

"There's a desert there?" Lexy cradled the phone between her ear and shoulder while she reached for the bakery box on the passenger seat, then she got out of the car and started across the parking lot.

Vera sighed. "You never heard of it? It used to be three hundred acres, but now it's about forty-five. You had better hurry if you want to see it, though. They say it will be gone in fifty years."

Lexy frowned at the phone. She'd never heard of any disappearing desert. "Gone? Where would it go?"

"The forest is reclaiming it," Vera said in an exasperated tone.

Lexy could hear clinking and muttering in the background as she opened the glass door and slipped into the lobby. "What's that noise in the background?"

"Oh, it's just your father."

"What's he doing?"

"Oh, he's just tinkering with the RV."

"Tinkering?" Lexy felt a wave of uneasiness wash over her. "Is something wrong with it?"

Silence.

"Mom?"

"It's just a little minor problem, Lexy. Nothing to worry about."

"Are you sure? I could send you some money—"

"Don't be silly! We don't need money ... your father's calling for me. I gotta go."

"Okay, Mom. Say hi to Dad and you guys take care."

"You, too. Say hi to Mona for us!"

Vera hung up and Lexy found herself standing outside Nans door, frowning down at her phone. Was something wrong with the RV? Nans had mentioned they'd been having trouble.

Her gut twisted—even though she'd offered to send her parents money, she'd been glad her mother had refused because she really didn't have any extra. She'd sunk every last dime into renovations at the bakery and was counting on the sale of Jack's house to replenish some of those funds and pay her parents back.

She raised her fist and knocked sharply on Nans' door. She really needed to kick this investigation into high gear—not only so she could clear Jack from the suspect list, but also so she could get the house sold and the money to help her parents.

***

"Lexy, come in." Nans opened the door and the smell of fresh-brewed coffee floated out into the hallway.

Ruth, Ida and Helen waved at Lexy from their seats around Nans' mahogany dining room table as she crossed the small foyer, then put the box in the center of the table.

"Coffee?" Nans asked from the small kitchen adjacent to the dining room.

"Yes, please." Lexy had rushed out of the house without her morning cup and had been too busy checking her rear-view mirror on the ride over to stop for coffee. She was practically comatose with lack of caffeine.

Ruth pulled out a chair and gestured for Lexy to sit while Nans shoved a mug in her hand. Lexy sipped the steaming brew gratefully.

"What did you bring?" Ida lifted the lid of the bakery box enthusiastically, her smile fading as she looked inside. "Don't you have any scones?"

Lexy narrowed her eyes. "No. Why? What's wrong with the cookies?"

The ladies exchanged a look. Ruth cleared her throat. Helen looked down at the floor. Nans got up and made herself busy in the kitchen.

"What?" Lexy repeated.

"Well, the meringues aren't bad," Ida said.

"But..." Lexy drew the word out.

"They just need more sugar," Ruth shrugged. "I'm sure they'd be perfect if they were just a bit sweeter."

"This is a new batch with more sugar than the last batch."

"Oh?" Ida raised her brows and the ladies all reached in and pulled out a cookie.

Lexy watched as Ida bit into hers and made a face. "Better try again, dear. Still needs more sweetener if you want to beat Violet."

Lexy's spirits sank. "More? I've upped the recipe twice now."

Ida glanced at the others and they nodded.

"Sorry, but it's better we tell you now so you can adjust," Ruth said.

"Yep, you know Violet won't make any mistakes with her meringue," Helen added.

"Speaking of Violet. Does she have a red Mustang convertible?" Lexy asked.

"Yes, I believe she does." Helen folded the half-eaten meringue cookie up in her napkin.

Ida nodded. "She won it in a slots tournament down at Foxwoods."

"Sheesh, is there nothing this woman doesn't win?" Lexy asked.

Ida, Ruth and Helen shrugged.

"Not that we know of," Ruth said. "What about you, Mona?"

"What?" Nans looked in from the kitchen, a yellow gingham dishtowel in her hand.

"Violet Switzer. Have you ever seen her lose anything?"

"Switzer ..." Nan scrunched up her face. "I'm not sure I know her."

"Sure, you do," Ruth said. "The one Ida is always complaining about."

"Oh, right. I don't know anything about her losing anything." Nans sat down at the head of the table. "Why are we talking about her?"

"Yeah, good question," Helen said. "We should be talking about the mummy case."

"Yes, let's get back to business," Ruth added."What's the plan?"

They looked at Nans, who shrugged. "Sorry, I don't really have one. I'm a bit out of the loop."

"Right," Ida took over. "Here's what we'll do. Mona, you and Lexy are going to talk to the McDonalds. Find out if the basement was bare blocks or had that cement stucco on it. Then maybe we'll know if O'Keefe was lying to us or not."

"Helen and I will use our 'resources' to see if there was any funny financial business going on with O'Keefe," Ruth said.

"Very good," Ida nodded. "Time is of the essence so we'll double up. Let's meet back here and figure out where to go after that."

"Sounds like a plan." Ruth stuck her fist out for a knuckle tap and the others did the same, then Lexy and Nans pushed back their chairs and started for the door.

Lexy opened the door and was just about to step out into the hall when she remembered something important. She turned to look at Ruth, Ida and Helen who were still seated at Nans table. "What about the cookies?"

The three women looked at each other and Ida made a face. "Sorry, dear. They still need more sugar."

***

Out in the hallway, Nans slowed to a crawl. She slipped on her crystal-studded fuchsia reading glasses and rummaged in her purse. "Why don't you go ahead and get the car. I need to make a quick call."

Lexy sensed Nans didn't want her listening in. Was she calling the mysterious boyfriend? Lexy couldn't help but smile. "Okay. I'll meet you out front."

Nans came out of the lobby doors just as Lexy pulled the car up, and they headed off in the direction of the McDonalds' senior living facility. Lexy was bursting with curiosity about this boyfriend that was causing Nans to act so secretive.

"Is there something you want to tell me?" Lexy asked.

Nans stiffened in her seat turning startled eyes on Lexy. "No. What do you mean?"

Lexy shrugged. "I heard you met a nice man …"

"Oh." Nans relaxed back into her seat, a smile curling her lips as she stared out the window. "Well, that's not anything I want to talk about right now."

"Oh, sorry." Lexy grimaced—she was dying to know about him but didn't want to invade Nans' privacy. Luckily, they'd reached the senior living facility and Lexy could change the subject.

"Have you been here? The place is pretty nice," Lexy said as they walked to the building together.

"Yes, I've visited them a few times." Nans held the door for Lexy, then proceeded in the direction of the McDonalds apartment.

"Do you visit them often?" Lexy asked.

Nans shrugged. "Not too often, but we still keep in touch a bit. All the old neighbors are still quite close."

"Oh, that's nice," Lexy said. "When I talked to them, they seemed a little ... umm ... forgetful."

"Well, that comes with the age. I visited them here not that long ago, and they seemed right as rain," Nans said as she rapped on the door.

The door opened almost immediately and Lois's face peered out, her eyebrows shooting up when she saw them. "Why, Mona, what a surprise! We haven't seen you in ages."

Nans frowned. "I was here the other day, Lois. Remember?"

"Oh, yes, of course. How silly of me. Time does get away from you at my age." She opened the door and gestured them in.

"Hi, ladies," Charles said from the recliner. "You'll pardon me if I don't get up. My hip is acting up today."

"Of course," Lexy said as she and Nans took seats on the couch.

Lois pulled a chair in from the kitchen and perched on the edge. "To what do we owe this pleasure?"

Nans nodded at Lexy, who said, "I had some questions about the basement in Jack's house ... your old house ... again."

"Oh, right. Terrible thing with that body and all." Lois clutched at Charlie's arm. "Do they know how it got there? Or when? Was it in our basement the whole time we lived there?"

"They're not sure yet," Lexy said. "But, we were wondering about the basement walls. The room was made by building a false wall and covering it with a cement coating. The builder said that the cinderblocks were exposed when he sold it to you. He said all the houses were that way."

Lois's eyes slide toward Nans and then Charlie. "Well, I don't know if I remember. It was so long ago."

"I checked my basement and it's cinderblock," Lexy said.

"Oh, no, we always kept it locked," Lois said. "No one could get in."

"No." Lexy raised her voice a few decibels. "I said cinderblock."

"Yes, I think they are made of cinderblock," Charlie said. "Unless you refinished them and they put some stucco cement coating on it to pretty it up."

"But was yours cinderblock when you moved in?" Lexy asked.

"I'm not sure." Charlie tapped the side of his head. "My memory isn't as good as it used to be. Do you remember, Mona?"

"I remember looking at it after you started the remodel and the walls were stucco, but I'm not sure if it was that way before," Nans said.

Lois's brows furrowed, causing wrinkles in her wrinkles. She looked at Lexy. "Why is this so important?"

"The builder claims the basement was raw cinderblocks when he sold it to you. I was thinking if you remembered that it was stucco when you moved in, it would prove he was lying and make him a suspect."

"Oh, dear." Lois looked at Nans. "Well, I wouldn't want to point the finger at someone who might be innocent if I wasn't sure. Did the police pinpoint the time of death to a date before we bought the house?"

"I haven't heard anything about an exact date, yet," Lexy said. "But it must have happened before you moved in—otherwise, surely you would have noticed."

"Yes, of course," Lois said. "Well, I'm sorry if we can't be much help. Our memories are not so good. And I feel just terrible this has happened in our old house ... and now you and George have to deal with it."

"Jack," Lexy said.

"Did you say track? I don't know if you're on the right track." Lois stood up. "If you could pinpoint the timeframe that person was killed, we might be able to help. It seems there was a stranger around the neighborhood and I wonder if he would have had something to do with it."

"You mentioned that before, but I don't see how it could be relevant to this case." Lexy followed Lois to the door.

"Now, don't be too hasty, dear," Nans said. "We need to consider every angle."

Lexy doubted that would be the case. How could a stranger possibly have made a secret room and put a body in the basement without the McDonalds knowing?

They said their goodbyes, and Lexy and Nans headed to the car. Nans seemed more interested in getting back to the retirement center in a hurry than she was in talking about the case, so the ride back was quiet. By the time Lexy dropped her off and headed back to the bakery, she was feeling a little down in the dumps.

Not only was Nans' lack of interest in the case disappointing, their trip to the McDonalds' hadn't given her any useful information, so she still had nothing concrete with which to nail Tom O'Keefe. She could only hope that her next stop would be more informative.

Chapter Nine

Cassie was knee deep in customers when Lexy arrived back at the bakery after dropping off Nans. She threw on an apron and rushed out front to help out. She sold several pies, dozens of cookies for take-out and countless scones and muffins for people who wanted to sit at the cafe tables and enjoy the view.

The constant rush of customers and chatter occupied her mind, leaving her no time to think about Nans or the mummy case.

Once the rush subsided, Lexy grabbed a white towel and made her way to the tables to clean up while Cassie re-arranged the bakery case.

"The ladies said my meringue recipe still needs sugar," Lexy complained as she wiped the crumbs from the table into her cupped hand.

"I didn't try the latest batch—"

Cassie stopped abruptly, causing Lexy to look up and see her friend looking at her funny ... no, not *at* her—over her shoulder. Lexy turned in the direction of Cassie's stare and her heart skidded when she saw a small, white-haired woman standing directly across the street. Not just any white hair woman. Lexy recognized her as the woman in the red Mustang—Violet Switzer.

Lexy's heart thudded as she realized Violet was staring straight at her. Their eyes met, then Violet raised two fingers, pointed them at her eyes, then extended her index finger toward Lexy.

I'm watching you.

Then she turned and disappeared into the haberdashery across the street.

"What the heck was that all about?" Cassie asked.

"That was Violet Switzer!"

"Your competition in the dessert contest?" Cassie's lips quirked up in a smile. "Looks like she's got you all riled up."

"Well, she's following me and it's creepy."

"Look, you're falling right into her trap. She's trying to psych you out. What you gotta do is pretend like it doesn't bother you."

Lexy chewed her bottom lip. Cassie was right. Violet was trying to get her all flustered and she was playing right in to her hands. "Yeah, you're right. I don't know why I'm letting her get to me. I mean, what's to be scared of? It's just a contest, for crying out loud."

"Right. Maybe you should turn the tables on her ... follow *her* around and see how she likes it," Cassie suggested.

"You know, that's a good idea." Lexy glanced across the street. Was Violet still in the store? Should she rush over and follow her? No, she didn't have time—she had more important matters to tend to. "I'll have to find out more about her. Maybe even pay her a visit ... but first, I have to stop in at *The Elms Pub.*

"*The Elms*?" Cassie frowned at Lexy. "Why do you have to go there?"

"Tom O'Keefe, the one who built Jack's house, used to hang around there and I was thinking I might be able to ask around about him. It seems like the kind of place that a lot of old-timers would still hang around at."

"Oh, it is," Cassie shut the bakery case door and moved over to the self-serve coffee station to straighten up the K-cups and pour a coffee for herself.

"You go there?" Lexy tossed her towel over her shoulder and crossed to the counter where she started to assemble a white bakery box.

"Yeah. My brother knows the owner—the grandson of the original owner, actually."

Lexy perked up. "You wouldn't be able to arrange for me to talk to the original owner, would you?"

"Pops? Sure, he's usually there every day. His name is Sam. Just tell him I sent you and he'll treat you like an old friend."

"Great." Lexy reached into the case and took out a tray of white, fluffy meringue cookies. "I'll take some of these meringues as a bribe."

"Is that the latest recipe?" Cassie asked.

Lexy nodded as she transferred the cookies in to the box.

"Let me try one." Cassie picked one off the plate. "We'll see if the ladies are right or if their taste buds are senile."

Lexy watched silently as Cassie took a bite, chewed, then licked her lips and nodded. "Sorry, they are right. It needs maybe just a touch of sugar— like only a teaspoon."

Lexy sighed. She'd have to carve out some time to fiddle with the recipe which meant less time on the case. Glancing out into the street where Violet had been, she felt her competitive nature take over. She knew she could win that dessert contest no matter what kinds of games Violet wanted to play. Besides, she could certainly best an old lady, both in cooking and psychology.

As far as Violet Switzer was concerned, it was game on. But first, Lexy had to find just one clue that would implicate Tom O'Keefe in the decades-old murder. She closed the lid of the box and headed out to *The Elms Pub*.

***

The Elms Pub sat on the corner of Elm and Center Streets across from the Mini-Mart gas station in the section of town where suburbia turned into small-town urban.

Lexy stood just inside the door, adjusting to the dim lighting. In front of her, a long, wooden bar ran half the length of the room. It was lined with high-backed bar stools, their brass footrests scuffed and black from years of use. Behind the bar, a few neon beer signs added extra lighting, which, in Lexy's opinion, was much needed.

Tables were scattered around the edge of the room. They looked clean and were mostly empty except for one table with two middle-aged men sipping beers and a booth in the back corner where a white-haired man cooled his palms around a frosted mug of golden liquid.

The bartender looking questioningly at Lexy's white box as she crossed to the bar.

"Hi." She smiled. "I'm looking for Sam. My friend, Cassie Darling, sent me."

"Oh, you know Cassie? She's a good friend. Pops is back there." He thrust his chin toward the white-haired man in the booth.

"Thanks."

Pops watched with curious eyes as Lexy made her way toward him. She stopped beside the booth, resting the bakery box on top of the table and holding out her hand. "Hi. I'm Lexy Baker, a friend of Cassie Darling."

His smile widened and he met Lexy's hand with a firm, warm handshake.

"I'm Sam Barlow. Any friend of Cassie's is a friend of mine." He gestured across the table. "Please sit."

Lexy slid into the booth just as the bartender appeared at her shoulder.

"Can I get you something?" he asked.

"Just a coffee, please."

"Comin' right up."

Sam nodded at the bakery box. "What's in there?"

"Meringue cookies. It's a new recipe I'm trying out for the Brook Ridge Desserts contest." Lexy flipped the top open and angled the box toward Sam so he could get a better look.

"Oh, you're the one that owns the bakery where Cassie works!" Sam said as he picked out a cookie.

"Yep. That's me. I don't know how well those go with beer, though."

Sam nodded, but bit in anyway. "It's good. But you didn't come all the way here to bring me cookies, did you?"

"No. I think you might be able to help me."

His brows raised a fraction of an inch, his gray eyes gleaming with interest. "How's that?"

"I'm sure you heard about the mummy that was found in one of the houses a few streets over."

Sam nodded.

"Well, that was my husband's house, and he's a suspect." Lexy watched as Sam grabbed another cookie. "I'd like to help clear his name."

"Why don't you have Cassie's young man help you? Isn't he a police detective?"

"Actually, he's my husband's partner. But they aren't allowed to investigate the case because the body was found in Jack's house ... and the detective on the case isn't being very cooperative."

Sam took a swig of beer and made a sour face. "You're right. Those cookies don't go very well with beer. Not sweet enough. Anyway, what makes you think I can help you?"

Lexy leaned across the table and lowered her voice. "Well, we have a theory that the killer is the builder that built all the homes in the neighborhood."

Sam's brows dipped into a 'V'. "You mean Tommy O'Keefe?"

"Yes."

"What makes you think that?"

"Because of the way the body was hidden. Someone made a secret room at the end of the basement—small enough so no one would notice it was ever there, and then they put the body in and sealed it off. That could only have been done before the home was occupied."

Sam rubbed his chin. "Not necessarily. If the homeowners were in on it, it could have been done at any time."

"It couldn't have been them," Lexy said. "They're a nice elderly couple!"

"Sure, *now* they are ... but back when those houses were built, they weren't old. You never know what people are up to."

Lexy tilted her head. He had a point. Still, what reason would the McDonalds have to hide a dead man in the basement?

A coffee appeared at her elbow and she slid it across the scarred wooden table until it was in front of her. "So, you don't think it was O'Keefe?"

Sam shrugged.

"You were here a lot back then, right?"

"Yeah. I ran the place. Couldn't afford much help back then so I was here all the time."

"Did you notice anything strange about O'Keefe back then? Or anyone else, for that matter." Lexy sipped her coffee and stared at him over the rim of her cup while he thought about it.

"Well, it was a long time ago and he *was* in here almost every night." Sam sipped his beer. "But I do seem to recall one time he bought rounds for the entire house."

Lexy's left brow ticked up. "Really? Did he say why?"

"Near as I can remember he said he'd made a big house deal. He was real excited about it."

"Do you remember exactly when that was?" Lexy asked.

Sam shook his head. "I can't recall the year, but I do remember it was summertime. Everyone was wearing t-shirts. I can picture it just like it was yesterday—everyone was pretty excited and we talked about it for weeks, since free drinks don't get offered often. Tommy was somewhat of a celebrity after that. Of course, he was already pretty well-known from the dart championships."

"I saw the trophies at his place."

"He won the championship a lot of years in a row."

"Until Violet Switzer came along."

Sam looked at her sideways. "You know her?"

"I don't actually know her. Just *of* her. I'm going up against her in the Brook Ridge Dessert contest." Lexy pointed to the box of cookies. "This is my test recipe for my entry in the contest."

Sam grimaced. "I don't envy you. That Violet can be a stickler. She likes to win, and once she has her mind set on something, she grabs on like a schnauzer's teeth biting the mailman's pant leg."

"Tell me about it."

"But the way to deal with people like her is to not let them intimidate you. Don't let her make you nervous." Sam picked another cookie out of the box and bit into it. "Add a little more sugar to this recipe and you've got a good shot."

Lexy's heart dropped thinking about the contest. Did she have a shot? She'd never had so much trouble with a recipe before. But she didn't have time to worry about that now—she had more important things to talk to Sam about than her cookie recipe. "So ... back to Tom O'Keefe. Did he have any enemies? Anyone he fought with?"

Sam shook his head. "Nope. Not at all. He was happy-go-lucky. Still is, actually. And no wonder, with all the money he's got." Sam narrowed his eyes at Lexy. "I don't get why you are so hell-bent on thinking it was Tommy. Do you have some compelling evidence that points to him?"

"I can't imagine who else would have been able to hide a body in the basement. It must have been done before the McDonalds moved in and, since he was the builder, he would have had the access to do that."

Sam shook his head. "This doesn't make sense to me. How did you discover it if it was a sealed off room and why did you never notice the room before?"

"The room was so narrow that no one would have noticed it was there unless they measured. Plus, the basement was full of piled up boxes so it was impossible to tell. It wasn't until we were cleaning it out and my dog scratched away some of the cement coating on the wall that we found a little hole and discovered the room."

"Did you say plaster on the walls?"

"Yeah. It was like some kind of plaster or stucco."

Sam nodded. "I know exactly what you mean. Seen that technique done in a lot of basements around here and I think that means you're barking up the wrong tree."

"How so?"

"Tommy didn't finish basements like that. If you think the killer is the one who did the cement job, then you don't want Tommy O'Keefe ... you want Bobby Nesbaum."

Chapter Ten

Lexy's cell phone chirped as she left *The Elms Pub*. But it wasn't Ida or Nans with the results of their financial search like she'd hoped—it was a text from her mother.

Lexy opened it to see a cock-eyed picture of a large, sandy area.

The Desert of Maine?

Lexy's heart pinched as she wondered if the reason her parents were still there was because they were having fun or because their RV broke and they couldn't go anywhere else. Judging by the picture, it didn't look like there was enough of anything to keep their interest for more than one day.

The best thing she could do to help them was to solve the case, so she let her thoughts turn toward what she'd learned from Sam.

Both Sam and Tom had said the basement renovator, Bobby Nesbaum, would have been the one do the wall treatment, but if Nesbaum had made a secret room and hidden a body in the basement, wouldn't Tom have noticed? Maybe the two of them were in on it together? Or, maybe Tom also knew how to put that cement on the walls and did it as a quick patch to hide the body. Maybe his plan all along was to frame Bobby if anyone discovered it.

By the time Lexy arrived at the bakery, her mind was whirling. She decided to focus on baking and filling the bakery cases. The day's rush of customers had made a big dent in the baked goods on display and she was happy to fill in the empty spaces with fresh-baked cookies, brownies and muffins.

She was bent over at the waist, her head inside the case, rearranging a plate of brownies when a familiar pair of blue-jean clad legs appeared on the other side of the glass front. Jack.

What was he doing here?

Lexy's stomach fluttered. Jack didn't usually visit her at the bakery unless it was something important. She pulled her head out of the case and stood, looking up at him from her five-foot-four high-heeled height.

"Hi." Jack smiled.

"What's wrong?"

"Nothing. Ida called and said to meet here and go over the clues. I just closed a case so I got off early today."

"Oh." Ida had called? Lexy pulled her phone out of the pocket of her apron and noticed she had a message from Ida.

Jack leaned against the case. "So, how did your meeting at the pub go?"

"Not that good ... I'll fill you in when the others are here."

As if on cue, the door opened, revealing Nans, Ruth, Ida and Helen. They made a beeline for the pastry case.

"Hi, there." The ladies murmured greetings and then got busy picking out pastries. Ruth chose a lemon tartlet, Helen, a brownie piled high with chocolate frosting, Nans, a fig square and Ida, a frosted chocolate cupcake top. Lexy noticed with dismay that none of them chose a meringue cookie.

They pulled two tables together and arranged the chairs around them. Then with pastries on napkins and steaming mugs of coffee and tea in front of them, they turn their attention to Nans.

"What?" Nans blinked.

"Well, aren't you going to start off?" Ida asked.

Nans broke off a piece of her fig square and paused with it in front of her mouth. "I don't know anything new, actually. Lexy and I went to the McDonalds' and they don't remember what their basement looked like so we couldn't say if Tom O'Keefe was telling the truth or not."

"What about his finances?" Jack asked.

"He did get some large sums of money that summer ... but it turns out that wasn't unusual," Helen said.

"We figure being a builder and all, he was probably transferring large sums between business and personal accounts all the time," Ruth added.

"He could have hidden the payoff and made it look like business." Ida's blue eyes sparkled at them over the rim of her teacup.

Jack narrowed his eyes at Helen and Ruth. "And just how do you ladies get this personal financial information? That stuff's not available to the general public."

Ruth's face turned pink and she waved her hand. "Oh, we have our ways."

Jack turned to Lexy. "What about your visit to the bar?"

"Sam didn't remember a lot. I mean, it *was* a long time ago. But he did remember Tom buying a couple of rounds for the entire bar one night. No one had ever done that before so it was memorable."

"Did Tom say why?" Ida asked.

"Sam said Tom had gotten a big contract to build some houses."

"And when was this?" Helen wiped chocolate frosting from her lips, then took another bite of the brownie.

"That's the thing. Sam didn't know. All he could remember was that it was in summer, because everyone was wearing t-shirts."

Jack looked skeptical. "You wouldn't think he'd want to advertise coming into a lot of money if he got a payoff to hide a body, though."

"Sam also said the same thing Tom did about the basement walls—Tom O'Keefe didn't finish them like that. He left the basements raw cinderblock."

"So, maybe Tom *was* telling the truth," Nans ventured.

"I'm sure Tom O'Keefe knows how to apply that cement coating to the walls. He's in the trade so he probably knows how to do a lot of things." Ida leaned forward. "He might even have done it on purpose to implicate Bobby Nesbaum if he was discovered."

"That's what I was thinking," Lexy said. Ida held her cup up and the two of them clinked rims.

"I'm sure it must have happened before the house was sold, so it must have been the builder," Ruth said.

"No matter what, we should check out this basement refinisher guy." Ida turned to Nans. "Mona, did you say he was dead?"

Nans looked up from the fig square she'd been pushing around her plate. "I ... well ... I think—

Just then, the door burst open and Watson Davies strode in, her blue eyes glaring at them. Her black biker boots clomped on the floor as she took two large strides over to the table.

"Good news, Jack." She stood with her feet apart, hands on hips, head tilted to the side looking down at Jack. Lexy thought her expression didn't look like that of one poised to impart 'good' news.

"Oh?" Jack looked up at her, his left brow ticking upwards a fraction of an inch.

"Yep, you're cleared off the suspect list. The M.E. pinpointed the time of death and it was quite some time before you bought the house."

Ida's brows shot up. "When was it?"

"August thirteenth, 1955."

"What? That's almost five years after the McDonalds moved in!" Ruth stared at Davies, then looked around the table at the rest of them.

"Wait a minute—they can pinpoint it down to the day?" Nans asked.

"Yes. And not only that, but we also know *who* the mummy is ... er ... was," Davies replied.

"Who?" Jack, Lexy, Ruth, Ida and Helen all asked at once.

"Earl Schute."

"Never heard of him." Ida said. "You know him, Mona?"

Nans pressed her lips together. "Schute ... it sounds vaguely familiar."

"It should," Davies tilted her head toward Nans. "Back in 1955, Earl Schute lived in the house right next door to you."

***

Silence descended on the bakery as they all stared at a red-faced Nans.

"Oh, well, now that you mention it, I guess I do remember him," Nans said sheepishly. "He didn't live there long, though, so I guess I didn't recognize the name right off."

"No, he didn't live there long." Davies agreed. "Because he was murdered. And it makes me wonder why no one in the neighborhood ever reported him missing."

Nans shrugged. "He kept to himself. We didn't see him a lot, so I guess no one noticed. I guess we just thought he moved away."

"So, what about my house? Can we go back in?" Jack asked.

"Not yet. We're still collecting evidence. "Lexy wilted as Davies speared her with a steely glare. "A task that would be easier if your dog hadn't run in and contaminated the crime scene."

Lexy grimaced. "Sorry."

Images of the receipt from *The Elms Pub* sprang to mind—maybe Sprinkles *had* gotten the receipt from the mummy. Should she tell Davies? Lexy glanced at the stern detective and figured she was better off not mentioning it unless she was positive it was a clue.

"So anyway, tell me about these McDonald characters," Davies was saying.

"Surely, you don't suspect them?" Nans sounded outraged.

"Of course I do. We found a dead body in their basement."

"Well ... I'm sure it wasn't them," Nans sputtered. "I mean, they're the nicest people, right Lexy?"

"They do seem very nice," Lexy replied.

"Right. That's what a lot of people say about killers." Davies produced a notepad from her back pocket and a pen from her front. Poising the pen over the pad, she asked; "Do you know where I can find them?"

Lexy rattled off the address. "But I've already talked to them and they don't know a thing about it."

"Playing detective again?" Davies asked, then turned to Nans. "What about you, Mona?"

"I'm not playing detective," Nans bristled. "Got too much else going on."

"Well, no matter. I'll have a little chat with them myself. I'm going to get to the bottom of this and find out what, *exactly,* went on in that neighborhood in the summer of 1955." Davies cast a suspicious glance at Nans, pivoted on her booted heel and left.

Chapter Eleven

"Well, how do you like them apples," Ida turned to Nans. "Mona, tell us all about this Earl guy. Who would want to kill him?"

"Obviously, the McDonalds did it," Ruth cut in.

Nans shook her head. "Not necessarily."

"Really?" Ruth screwed up her face at Nans. "The body was in their basement, so they must have done it or been a party to it."

"Not if they weren't home at the time." Nans picked her giant purse up from the floor and put it in her lap. Snapping open the clasp, she plunged her hand into the cavernous opening.

"You expect us to believe someone broke into their house and hid the body, then redid their basement while they were out to dinner?"

"Of course not," Nans retorted as she rummaged inside the purse. "No one could do that in one night. But now that we know the exact date, I seem to recall that was the summer the McDonalds went to Europe. They were gone for a whole month."

"Wouldn't they have noticed that someone redid their basement when they got home?" Helen asked.

"That's the thing. They were having the basement redone that summer. That was one of the reasons they planned the trip—it was perfect timing to get away from the construction." Nans shrugged. "Someone could have used that as a convenient way to hide the body."

"This still doesn't add up," Jack cut in. "Even if the McDonalds were in Europe, one of the neighbors would have noticed something."

'That's right," Ida said. "Surely, it would smell. Did you notice anything funny over there, Mona? Any odd activity or a funny smell?"

"No, but I wouldn't have, because that summer was when the Fergusons' toddler flushed Lego's down the toilet and their septic system backed up all over the back yard." Nans wrinkled her nose. "Boy, did that create a stench. The whole neighborhood walked around holding their noses for weeks."

"Would that cover the smell of a dead body?" Lexy asked Jack.

Jack nodded. "And even if it didn't, who would be able to differentiate?"

"So, I guess this puts Tommy O'Keefe in the clear," Ruth said.

"But implicates Bobby Nesbaum," Helen added.

"Or the stranger," Nans cut in.

"Stranger?" Ida, Ruth, Helen and Jack looked at Nans.

Nans nodded. "Yeah, you remember we talked about that at the McDonalds', Lexy?"

Lexy did remember them mentioning it. "But how would a stranger know the McDonalds were away and how would they gain access to the basement?"

"Not to mention, how would they make the secret room and close it up without Bobby Nesbaum noticing," Jack added.

"Well, it seems all fingers point to Nesbaum." Ruth pulled her purse off the back of her chair and rummaged inside, pulling out an iPad, which she placed on the table in front of her.

"Either it was him or he was in cahoots with someone," Helen offered.

"Someone who knew the McDonalds were gone," Lexy said.

"And who would know that?" Ruth asked.

Ida snapped her fingers. "The other neighbors!"

"That's right. And a lot of them still live in the neighborhood. I'll talk to some of them tonight when I get home. Do you want to come with me, Nans?" Lexy turned to Nans, who stood there with her cell phone in her hand.

"What?" Nans glanced up from the cell phone display. "Sorry, I have some stuff going on tonight and right now I have to warn the McDonalds that Davies is coming!"

Ida stared after Nans who had walked to the other side of the bakery to make her phone call, then turned back to the group at the table. "Never mind her—we need to divvy up the assignments."

"Right," Helen said and they all leaned forward.

"What do you suggest, Jack?" Ida asked.

Jack shrugged. "Well, I guess I'd check out this Nesbaum character, first of all."

"If he's even still alive. I believe Mona said he had passed on," Helen mumbled around the last bite of her brownie.

"Nope. He's alive." Ruth slid the iPad into the center of the table and pointed to a blurb of text on the display. "Says right here he still lives in town."

"Well, it's good to know Mona isn't right about everything." Ida glanced uneasily across the room at Nans. "Still, I wonder if she's feeling okay. She seems a might distracted."

Ruth snickered. "It's probably that new boyfriend of hers."

"Or the fact that Davies might see her as a suspect now," Jack said.

Lexy chewed her bottom lip. "That's silly. Nans wouldn't have had anything to do with that. Why, back then, my grandpa was still alive and he was a cop!"

"Well, Davies might not see it that way. You know how she is." Ruth rolled her eyes. "Anyway, Helen and I will check out this Bobbie Nesbaum online and see if he got a big influx of money or if there're any news articles about him."

"Jack, maybe you can feel Davies out. Maybe she'll be more forthcoming with information on the case now that you aren't a suspect," Ida said.

Jack laughed. "I doubt that, but I'll try."

"And I'll ask around the neighborhood to see what some of the old neighbors know about Earl Schute," Lexy offered.

Sounds like a plan." Ida brushed the crumbs from her fingers onto her plate and then looked up at Lexy. "But you'd best be careful because one of those neighbors could be a cold-blooded killer!"

***

"Earl Schute was the kind of guy who brought trouble with him wherever he went," Ed Johnston said as he munched on one of Lexy's meringue cookies, his eyes narrowed at the house next to Lexy's—the house Earl Schute once lived in.

Lexy had figured the elderly Mr. Johnston would be a wealth of information. He'd lived in the neighborhood forever and surveyed the goings-on from his porch daily. Lexy had run across the street to his house as soon as she'd gotten home from the bakery, and now they sat on twin rocking chairs enjoying a light summer evening breeze as Lexy picked his memory.

"What do you mean?" Lexy asked.

"He wasn't a pleasant person ... was always stirring up trouble."

"What kind of trouble?"

"Well, for example, he didn't keep that house very nice. Had trash all over the lawn and he put up a fence halfway into the neighbor's yard. I know your grandpa had a few words with him and Floyd Nichols on the other side almost came to blows with him one night out in the street." Ed chuckled at the memory.

"Really?" Lexy's nerves tingled. Could Floyd Nichols be the killer? But how would he have gotten the body into the McDonalds' basement and closed it up in that little room? Maybe he killed Earl and then hired Nesbaum to help him?

"Anyway, I tried to steer clear of him," Ed said.

"So, you didn't notice when he disappeared?"

"Disappeared? No. Well, I did notice the neighborhood was more pleasant, and then one day I realized it was because he wasn't here picking fights. But I couldn't pinpoint an exact day when he wasn't here anymore."

"You heard about the body at the McDonalds?"

"Yeah, creepy." Ed picked another cookie out of the white bakery box Lexy had given him. "These are good."

"Really?" Lexy's hope rose. "You don't think they need more sugar?"

Ed swallowed the cookie and pressed his lips together. "Maybe. Hard to say. Anyway, the body at the McDonalds' ... how'd it get in there?"

"That's what I'm trying to find out." Lexy looked at him out of the corner of her eye. "That's why I was asking about Earl."

Ed's eyes widened. "You mean it was Earl in there?"

"Yep."

"Lois and Charlie killed Earl?"

"No, no. I mean, I don't think so. The police say he died in the summer of 'fifty-five and Nans said the McDonalds were away that summer."

Earl squinted up at the evening sky. "They did go away one summer ... I can't remember the exact year, but I remember they traveled to Europe because they came back and Lois stunk up the whole neighborhood with some spicy cooking. Indian, I think."

Stunk up the neighborhood? That reminded Lexy of the septic system. "Nans said something about one of the neighbors' septic systems backing up that summer, too."

"I don't recall that. Could be. If it was over on your side of the street, I might not have smelled it. Who was it?

"The Fergusons."

"Oh, yeah, they were on the same street as the McDonalds, but down a few houses." Ed shrugged. "I'm glad I didn't have to smell *that*—it can be right awful. Lois's cooking was bad enough."

"Nans also said something about some stranger that was in the neighborhood that summer."

Ed thought for a bit, then said, "I don't remember no stranger. 'Course I don't spend all my time on the porch watching the neighborhood like some people think."

"Of course not," Lexy soothed. "But you did see Floyd Nichols fighting with Earl?"

"Yeah, sure as day, right out in the street—fists up and everything."

"Do you know what they were fighting about?"

Ed shrugged. "Could have been lots of things. I think I heard Floyd yelling about the fence, though."

"And did you see Earl around after that?"

"What? Hmmm ... well, I don't know. It was shortly after that, I think, I noticed the neighborhood was a lot quieter, and then I realized I hadn't seen Earl in a while."

"Didn't anyone notice that Earl just went missing?"

"No. Who would care? I think people were relieved, what with the insurance scam and all."

Lexy's eyes widened. "Insurance scam?"

"Yeah, would you believe Earl was passing himself off as a life insurance agent? Took money from half the neighborhood." Ed clucked and shook his head. "Of course, I didn't fall for it, but some others lost several thousand, and that was a lot of money in those days."

"Was Floyd one of them?"

I think so, and I think the McDonalds were, too. Hey, come to think of it, that's right around the time Earl disappeared ..." Ed turned to Lexy, realization dawning on his face, "... you don't think one of them killed him over it, do you?"

Chapter Twelve

Lexy left Ed with the box of cookies on his porch, her head spinning with information. Could Floyd Nichols have killed Earl over the property disagreement? Or did Earl's death have something to do with the insurance scam? And what, if anything, did Nans know about those things?

Ed had said Lexy's grandfather had had words with Earl, too, but Nans had acted like she barely remembered Earl ... either Nans knew more than she was letting on, or her memory was going. Lexy's heart pinched at the thought—was Nans lack of enthusiasm about the case due to a memory problem and not a boyfriend?

Lexy had tried to get some answers by rushing over to Floyd's as soon as she'd left Ed, but no one answered the door. There was no car in the garage, either. She'd have to come back later.

At home, she found Jack in the kitchen putting the finishing touches on a salad. Sprinkles sat at his feet, watching his every move.

"What did you find out?" He pecked her cheek, then reached around her to grab a plate of thick, juicy steaks from the fridge.

Lexy eyed the steak, her mouth watering as she told Jack about her conversation with Ed Johnston.

"An insurance scam?" Jack salted and peppered the steaks, then nodded toward the kitchen door. "Get that for me, will you?"

Lexy opened the door and followed him out onto the patio, watching as the steaks sizzled on the hot grill. The smell of grilling meat made her stomach growl and she realized she'd forgotten to eat lunch.

"Yeah, Ed said Earl was running some kind of life insurance scam and ripped off a bunch of the neighbors."

Jack's brows shot up. "That sounds like serious stuff. Nans didn't mention that. Do you think she knows?"

"She must know. I mean, she's usually up on everything that's going on, plus Ed said that Grampy had words with Earl more than once." Lexy chewed her bottom lip. "I don't know if they had words about the insurance scam, but it seems like Nans must know more than she's letting on. Do you think she knew about the insurance scam and didn't say anything?"

"Probably not. I mean, people don't usually talk about finances like that. Especially back then." Jack walked past her to the door. "Help me get the plates and salad."

Lexy relaxed. Jack was right. Nans probably really didn't remember Earl—it was over fifty years ago that he was around. She was probably blowing things out of proportion and worrying about nothing.

She followed Jack back into the kitchen and he loaded her up with plates, napkins, salad bowls and the salad, then reached into the fridge and pulled out a bottle of wine and grabbed two glasses from the counter.

"I got the important stuff." Jack gestured to the wine bottle as he opened the door for her.

"So, what do you plan to do next?" Jack asked after they were settled at the patio table with their food.

"I guess I need to talk to Floyd next. I went over there after Ed's but he wasn't home." Lexy cut off a slice of steak, the inside perfectly pink and the outside just charred—exactly the way she liked it. She paused, her steak-laden fork in front of her mouth. "Did you find anything out from Davies?"

Jack shook his head. "No, she's clammed up. All she would tell me was that the McDonalds verified they were on Vacation that summer and then they mentioned the stranger Nans was talking about—a tall guy with long hair."

"I asked Ed about him, but he didn't remember any stranger." Lexy speared a tomato and nibbled the edge.

"It's a very odd case. It seems no one reported this guy missing." Jack topped off Lexy's glass of wine and then his own. "I mean, didn't the guy have any family?"

"Judging by what Ed said about him, I doubt it. He sounded like a jerk, so maybe he was estranged from his family."

"Woof." Sprinkles looked up at Lexy ... or rather, at the piece of steak on the end of Lexy's fork. The dog's pleading, brown eyes won her over and she took the piece and held it out to the dog who inhaled it.

"I do think it's kind of funny that Sprinkles messed with Davies' crime scene. Serves her right for being so mean," Lexy said, remembering the receipt from *The Elms Pub*. "I should probably ask Sam down at the pub if he knew Earl. I didn't know the identity of the mummy when I talked to him before."

"It's worth a try," Jack agreed. "Hopefully, Ruth and Helen can dig up some information on him and maybe Nans will remember something."

"Yeah, I need to talk to her, too. I tried to call but she's not answering."

"Probably out with that new boyfriend," Jack teased. "Have you met him?"

"No, I tried to get information on him but Nans said she didn't want to talk about it yet."

"Well, now that I'm not the main suspect anymore, maybe you don't have to spend so much time on the mummy case. You do have that dessert contest to prepare for, don't you?"

Lexy's heart sank. She did have to get going with her recipe—the contest was in a few days. And she had Violet Switzer to deal with. But with all the running around she needed to do, when was she going to find time for that?

Solving the mummy case was important, too. She needed the money from the sale of Jack's house to pay her parents back. Her chest squeezed as she thought about them. She wanted to call and ask if they needed money for the RV, but she knew they wouldn't tell her if they did. The only way to make sure they would actually take money from her was to repay the loan.

Lexy steeled herself with another glass of wine. She'd better get a good night's sleep. Tomorrow was going to be a busy day.

Chapter Thirteen

The next day, Lexy woke to see a cloudless, blue summer sky peeking out from between the gap in her bedroom curtains. She stretched lazily and pushed the curtains apart for a full view.

She looked out the window. Her heart jumped! A red car was parked right in front of her house—Violet Switzer's Mustang!

She pressed her face to the window in time to see a little, white-haired lady sprinting across her front lawn.

Lexy took the stairs two at a time, the squealing tires of the Mustang echoing in her ears as she reached the bottom step.

She ripped the front door open.

The car was gone. A white bakery box sat on the top step.

Lexy stepped out onto the stoop, looking up and down the street for a sign of Violet, but she was long gone. Her gaze dropped to the bakery box.

What could possibly be in there?

Lexy felt a niggle of trepidation as she bent down, picking the box up gingerly and bringing it inside.

"What's going on?" Jack asked from the middle of the staircase he'd been descending.

"I had a visit from my competitor."

"That Violet person?"

"Yep." Lexy held the box up. "She left this."

Jack eyed the box suspiciously. "Should we open it? She's not the type that blows up her competition, is she?"

"I hope not." Lexy knew Jack was joking, but her heart skittered as she slowly pried open the lid with the tip of her fingernail.

Inside were smashed up meringue cookies—her cookies. And a note.

"These will never beat my pies. You might as well quit now and save yourself the humiliation." Lexy read the note to Jack.

Jack made a face. "Are you going to let her intimidate you like that?"

"Heck, no." Lexy tossed the box on the table. "This is a battle ... Violet may have fired the first shot, but I intend to win the war!"

Lexy ran up the stairs, showered and got ready in record time. She didn't know how, but somehow she was going to give Violet a taste of her own medicine. She needed to find out where Violet lived in order to do that. And she needed to make a little adjustment to her recipe—if everyone wanted more sugar in those cookies, that's what they'd get.

But first she needed to talk to Floyd Nichols.

***

Lexy punched the doorbell of the white ranch home and wiped her sweaty palms on her jeans.

Why was she so nervous?

Oh, yeah, because she was about to interrogate a neighbor who might have killed someone and shoved them in another neighbor's basement, that's why.

The door opened and the wrinkly face of Floyd Nichols looked out at her.

"Lexy Baker?"

"Yes. Hi, Mr. Nichols."

"Come on in." He opened the door and Lexy stepped into the living room. Like many of the older neighbors, Floyd Nichols hadn't felt the need to remodel or even buy new furniture in over thirty years. It was almost like stepping back in time—an orange floral couch sat on one wall, an avocado green recliner across from it. The only item that had been updated was the large flat screen TV which wobbled on a flimsy particle board stand in the corner.

"Please, have a seat." He gestured toward the recliner and then picked up the remote and muted the volume of the TV. "What can I do for you?"

Lexy cleared her throat. *Where to start?*

"I guess you heard what happened over at Jack's house ... the McDonalds' old house?"

"Yes, of course." Nichols sat on the couch, leaning forward with his forearms on his knees and looked expectantly at her.

"I wasn't sure if you knew who it was."

Nichols eyes flashed surprise. "The body? What would make you think I would know who it was?"

"I didn't know if you'd seen it on the news yet. It was an old neighbor. Earl Schute."

Nichols leaned back into the couch. "Oh, you don't say? I remember Earl."

Lexy studied Nichols' face as she said, "I was wondering if you could tell me anything about him. I know he lived next door to you."

"Yeah. He did. In between me and your grandparents." Nichols' face turned sour. "Earl wasn't very easy to get along with."

"I heard. I also heard you got into a fight with him."

Nichols narrowed his eyes. "Now, who told you that?"

Lexy shrugged. "Another neighbor. I also heard he had some insurance scam going. Was that why you were fighting?"

"Insurance scam?" Floyd shook his head. "Nope, not me. We fought because Earl kept putting his junk in my yard. But I wasn't the only one around here that fought with him. He could be right obnoxious, especially after he'd been hanging around at that bar."

Lexy straighten in her chair, remembering the receipt Sprinkles had found. "You mean *The Elms Pub*?"

"Yep. Lots of people went there back then. The town wasn't as built up and it was the only watering hole for quite a ways." Nichols crossed his ankle over his knee. "Anyway, why all the interest?"

Lexy sighed. "The police have Jack's house closed up until they solve the case and we need to put it on the market to sell. I'm just trying to help the case along."

"So, you're wondering if I have any ideas as to who killed him?"

"Yep. The McDonalds are prime suspects for obvious reasons, but Nans says there's no way they did it."

"Oh, no." Nichols shook his head. "Not Lois and Charlie. They wouldn't hurt a fly. Besides, they were away in Europe that summer."

"Yeah, that's what Nans said. Do you remember anything unusual, any odd things going on over at their house? A weird smell?"

"Of course. That was the summer someone's septic system overran. It was ripe, I tell you." Nichols looked up at the ceiling, chuckling at the memory. Then he stopped laughing, leaned slightly forward and fixed Lexy with a serious look. "But that's not the strangest thing. That summer, a stranger was seen around town. I saw him on the street with my own eyes. We hardly ever had strangers hanging around."

"Really? What did he look like?"

Nichols answered without hesitation, as if the image of the stranger was burned in his memory. "He was short and stocky. Muscular with a dark beard and beady eyes. Just the kind of guy that would hide a body in someone's basement while they were on vacation."

***

Lexy left Floyd Nichols' house with a sneaking suspicion that he knew more about Earl Schute's death than he was letting on. It was no secret that the two men had fought, but that was probably no reason to suspect Floyd since it sounded like lots of people fought with Earl.

The thing that worried Lexy was that she hadn't told Floyd what year Earl had died. Floyd had claimed he hadn't seen anything about it on the news —that's why he didn't know the mummy was Earl. But if that were the case, how could he have possibly known it was the same year the McDonalds were in Europe?

Lexy hated to do it, but she moved Floyd Nichols to the top of her suspect list.

Nichols had claimed he didn't know about the insurance scam, but he could have been lying ... and something about his mention of the stranger seemed odd to Lexy but she couldn't quite place it. Maybe she'd find out more at *The Elms Pub*.

On the way to the pub, Lexy tried to call Nans but there was no answer, so she called Ida.

"This is Ida." Ida answered the phone like she was running a business.

"Hi, Ida, it's Lexy. I tried to call my grandmother, but she didn't answer."

"She's gone out in Ruth's car again."

"Oh." Lexy felt that familiar pang of worry.

Ida must have read her thoughts. "Now, don't you worry. She's just man-crazy. You know how it can be."

"Right. Of course." Lexy pushed aside her worry and brought her thoughts back to the case. "Did you find anything on Nesbaum?"

"Not a thing. He's clean as a whistle. We plan to pay him a personal visit tomorrow, though. You in?" Ida asked.

"Absolutely," Lexy replied. "I'm on my way to *The Elms Pub*. My neighbor told me Earl hung out there."

"Oh, that's interesting. Tom O'Keefe did, too." Ida paused. "But I guess we've already ruled O'Keefe out, what with the timeline and all. What else did you find out from the neighbors?"

"I guess Earl wasn't well-liked. In fact, one neighbor saw another neighbor fighting with him in the street."

"Oh, that sounds promising." Ida's voice carried a hopeful lilt.

"Well, normally I would say so, too, but all the neighbors fought with Earl ... including my grandfather."

"Mona's husband?"

"Yep."

"But I thought Mona barely remembered Earl."

"That's what she said, but she also said Nesbaum was dead. I'm a little worried her memory is failing."

"Mona? No. She's still sharp as a tack. It's her hormones—she's gone dumb over this guy. It can be that way, you know. Why, I remember when I met my Norm, we used to sneak away and—"

"One of my neighbors also mentioned that Earl was running some kind of insurance scam," Lexy cut in. She didn't want to hear about what Ida and Norm used to do when they snuck away, much less picture her grandmother doing similar things with this new boyfriend.

"Scam? Oh, my, the plot thickens."

"Tell me about it." Lexy turned into the parking lot of *The Elms*. "I'm at the pub so I gotta run. Maybe you guys could do your magic and look into Earl's financials to see if there's any truth to this insurance scam?"

"We're on it," Ida said. "How 'bout you swing by the retirement center right after your visit and we can compare notes."

"Sounds good. See you then."

The bar was empty except for the bartender who was arranging the liqueur bottles behind the bar, facing away from her. Lexy shifted her eyes to the booth in the back, disappointed to see it empty. Sam wasn't there. Her eyes darted up to the clock—no wonder—it wasn't even nine o'clock!

The bartender turned and Lexy noticed it was the same guy from the previous day.

His brows ticked up. "Back again, eh?"

"Yeah." Lexy smiled sheepishly. "I didn't realize how early it was. I was hoping to catch Sam."

"We're not really open, but Gramps is in the pool room out back." The bartender thrust his chin toward a dark opening in the back of the bar. "Go ahead back. I know he enjoyed talking to you the other day."

Lexy made her way tentatively toward the opening. Peering in, she saw two pool tables side by side, dartboards on the wall and various tables with chairs resting upside down on top of them. Much to her surprise, Sam was swishing a large mop around the floor, a yellow-wheeled bucket beside him.

"They put you to work for your beer?" Lexy asked from the doorway.

Sam squinted up at her, his face cracking into a smile as he recognized her. "Well, hi there. Lexy, right?"

Lexy nodded.

"Come on in." Sam took two wooden chairs down from one of the smaller tables and pulled one out for her to sit in. "Watch out for the wet floor there."

Lexy deftly stepped over the wet area and sat in the chair. Sam sat in one opposite her. "So, to what do I owe this pleasure?"

"I had some more questions about the mummy in the basement. If you don't mind."

"Mind? Heck, no. Not too many people come by to ask me questions anymore. Whatcha wanna know?"

"I don't know if you saw on the news, but they found out who it was. I heard he used to come in here. A guy by the name of Earl Schute."

Sam's eyes widened. "Earl Schute. He's the mummy? Well, I'll be."

"You knew him." Lexy said it as a statement more than a question.

"Oh, sure. He came in here quite a bit at one time. Troublemaker. I'm not surprised someone killed him."

"Did he cause trouble with anyone in particular?"

"I don't think he played favorites. As I recall, he was mean to everyone."

"Did he know Bobbie Nesbaum?"

Sam shrugged. "I think they both came here around the same time. Of course, it's all kind of fuzzy now. That was years ago. But I don't remember them being friends. I don't remember Earl being friends with anyone."

"Yeah, that's the impression I get," Lexy said. "Do you remember any strangers in the bar ... people coming in and asking about Earl?"

"Well, there're always strangers coming in along with the regulars." Sam puckered his lips and looked up at the ceiling. "I don't remember anyone asking about him, though, except Violet."

Lexy's brows shot up. "Violet Switzer?"

"Yep. That's right. I remember you said you're going up against her in some competition."

"Yes, the Brook Ridge Dessert competition." Lexy's stomach twisted. She really needed to get going on her meringue recipe. "But why was Violet asking about Earl?"

"Well, at first I thought she might have the hots for him, but then I realized a woman like her probably didn't get the hots for anyone. Though they would have made the perfect couple—both of them being so nasty and all." Sam shrugged. "Anyway, I just figured they must have been competing in some contest and Violet wanted to get info on him."

"What contest?"

"She didn't say."

"Did Violet come here a lot?"

"Nah, only for the dart and pool tournaments."

Lexy remembered the trophies on O'Keefe's mantle and wondered how many different trophies Violet had on *her* mantle. "So, you don't know if she lives around here."

"Oh, sure ... well, she used to. Used to live right down in The Elms. On Oak Drive, I believe."

Lexy stared at Sam in shock. "Oak Drive?"

"Yeah. I'm pretty sure."

Oak drive was the street that intersected with Lexy's. Nans *must* have known Violet—as far as Lexy knew, her grandmother had made it her business to know everyone within a two-mile radius of her former home.

And now, Lexy had another person to add to her suspect list—Violet. Which was just as well since she had to talk to Violet about the contest, anyway. She might as well ask her a few questions about Earl while she was at it. "You said she used to live there. Does that mean she doesn't anymore?"

"Nope. She came into some money and lives up on Chapel Hill now," Sam said, referring to the ritzy section of town.

Lexy's eyes narrowed. "Really? When did she come into this money?"

"Oh, years ago."

"Around nineteen-fifty-five?"

"It could have been around then. It was a long time ago. Do you think she had something to do with Earl gettin' killed?"

"Maybe." Lexy *wanted* to think she did because it was starting to look like Earl's death might have something to do with one of her neighbors and she'd much rather have it be Violet. Her coming into money around the time of Earl's death was suspicious, but it still didn't explain how Violet could have gotten him into the McDonalds' basement or *why* she would have killed him.

Sam leaned across the table. "I wouldn't put murder past that woman, but if you asked me who would have wanted to kill Earl, I'd say it was Paddy Sullivan."

Lexy reared back in shock. Paddy and his wife, Mary, had lived on Jack's street since she was a little girl. They were good friends with Nans. "Paddy Sullivan? Why?"

"Earl had his eye on Paddy's wife, Mary. Made quite a few passes at her in front of everyone. Paddy's got an Irish temper if I ever did see one, and he didn't like that at all. Almost punched Earl out right here in the bar. 'Course I stopped that from happening." Sam raised his right arm, flexed his pale, thin bicep and shrugged with a sheepish grin on his face. "I used to be more buff back then."

Lexy laughed along with Sam, but her heart wasn't really in it. Now she had a new suspect to add to her list and another neighbor to interrogate.

Paddy Sullivan.

Chapter Fourteen

Lexy's shoulders slumped as she walked into the Brook Ridge Retirement Center. Her conversations with Floyd and Sam had been enlightening, but she felt a feeling of foreboding that most of the clues pointed to her elderly neighbors.

"Yoo-hoo, Lexy!" Ida's voice boomed from across the room, pulling her from her thoughts. She headed toward the table where the three ladies were sitting, her heart sinking even lower when she realized Nans was not with them.

"Where's Nans?"

"Still not back." Ruth pulled out a chair and Lexy sat.

"We didn't have much luck with our searches." Helen peered at Lexy over the tops of her half-moon glasses. "What about you?"

"I'm not sure if you'd say I had 'luck', but I did get some new information. It's too bad what I found out has me more confused than anything else."

"What did you find out?" Ruth asked.

"Earl did hang around there," Lexy answered. "And it turns out he was a jerk there, too."

"Did your contact say if there was anyone in particular who might have wanted him dead?"

"Not really, but interestingly enough, he said that Violet Switzer had been asking around about Earl."

"Violet?" Ida's face wrinkled in distaste. "Were they competing in a contest?"

"He didn't know."

"Would Violet kill to win a contest?" Ruth asked.

"So far, she hasn't had to," Helen answered. "She just annoys people so much that they lose because they are so rattled."

"Speaking of which," Lexy said. "I heard she used to live in my neighborhood and has since moved to Chapel Hill."

"That's right," Ida said. "She must have won enough prizes she could afford one of them fancy houses."

"Or got a big pay-off for something ..." Lexy suggested.

"You don't think she had something to do with Earl, do you?" Ruth asked.

Lexy shrugged. "It's probably just wishful thinking because my other suspects are all people I know, but she did come into some money to move to Chapel Hill. I just don't know when or if it could be related to Earl's strange death."

"Well, it's easy enough to find out when she moved." Ruth whipped an iPad out of her purse, placed it on the table and started typing. A few seconds later, she said, "Yep, she bought that house in the beginning of nineteen-fifty-six."

"Ha! I knew she was ruthless!" Ida said. "She must have known he was gonna beat her in some contest and she did away with him."

"Now, Ida, that's speculation," Helen said. "Intimidating people to win a contest is one thing, but killing them is quite another. No one does that."

"At least we better hope not, or Lexy might be next on her list," Ruth added.

Lexy frowned. "I was planning to visit her later ..."

Helen held up her hand. "Wait, this doesn't make sense. She couldn't have killed Earl and put him in the basement by herself. This isn't about winning a contest. There's got to be more to it."

That made Lexy feel a little better. She wanted to win the dessert contest, but she wasn't *dying* to win it.

"So, you think she had an accomplice? Who?" Ruth asked.

"Maybe it wasn't her. Let's not get fixated on that, even though I really want it to be her," Ida said. "We need to explore all our clues methodically, like we do with every case."

"Did you guys find out anything about the insurance scam?" Lexy asked. "It seems more likely it has something to do with that than with a contest."

Ruth shook her head. "We didn't find a thing. Literally. Earl Schute had no bank accounts."

"What? That's odd."

"Yeah. Not only that, but he seems to be a ghost."

"A ghost?"

Ruth made a face. "It's almost as if he didn't exist before nineteen-fifty-five. The first thing I can find about him online is a listing at the address on your street. He didn't buy that house though, he rented."

Lexy stared at Ruth. "Even so, he must have had a bank, especially back in the fifties where there weren't any online payments or many credit cards. People needed to write checks back then, didn't they? How did he cash his paycheck without having a bank account?"

"He didn't get a paycheck."

"What? He must have worked somewhere?"

"Can't find any record of a job."

"Well, that *is* strange. How did he get money?"

"Apparently, he scammed it out of people," Ida said.

"I wouldn't think that would be enough to make a living." Lexy tapped her finger on the table. "So all we know is he hung around the neighborhood being a nuisance and he went to the pub."

"Where he was also a nuisance," Helen pointed out.

"And scammed people out of money," Ruth added. "Did your contact at the bar have any other information?"

"He said one of my neighbors, Paddy Sullivan, had an ongoing problem with Earl."

"Paddy Sullivan? Doesn't he live a few houses down from Jack?" Ida asked.

Lexy nodded. "Sam said Earl used to make passes at Paddy's wife and it made Paddy pretty mad. He mentioned something about them fighting over it in the bar."

Ida's left brow ticked up. "Jealousy is one of the prime motives for murder."

"I know," Lexy said. "But I can't believe nice old Mr. Sullivan would *kill* someone. Fighting's one thing ... murder is another."

"Very true." Ruth pulled up a document on the iPad. "Now, let's go over the suspects and clues."

"Well, there's Violet," Ida said. "My money's on her. She was asking about him in the bar and she lived in that neighborhood."

"Then there's the neighbor you just mentioned," Helen said. "Paddy Sullivan."

"And my other neighbor, Floyd Nichols," Lexy added. "He was seen fighting with Earl and I already know he lied to me."

"Let's not forget about the McDonalds," Helen cautioned. "After all, the body was found in their basement. We should check that they really *were* in Europe."

"And then there's the stranger that people keep referring to," Lexy said. "Maybe we should see if there are any newspaper articles or police reports about him."

"Good idea. I'll note that as an action item." Ruth's gnarled fingers flew along the surface of the iPad.

"And we still need to talk to this Bobby Nesbaum. He had access to the basement and was refinishing it, so he's *got* to be involved somehow," Ida said.

"This is all so confusing," Helen sighed. "I feel like a big piece is missing."

"The thing that is missing," Ida said, "is motive. We need to figure out *why* someone killed him. Then it should be easy to figure out who the killer is."

Lexy's phone chirped, notifying her of a text, and she looked at the screen. "It's Jack. He says he has some new clues and wants to meet with us later at the bakery."

"Good, that's just what we needed," Ruth said.

"Yeah, I could go for some scones and maybe a brownie," Ida added.

"No, I mean the new clues." Ruth swatted Ida in the arm and they all laughed.

"I could use the clues *and* the pastry," Helen said. "And hopefully, Mona will show up. She lived in the neighborhood and knows all the people involved. I'm sure she can shed some light on this case."

Chapter Fifteen

Lexy squeezed a blob of pink, creamy meringue out of the piping bag onto the parchment-lined tray, guiding it carefully so that the result was shaped like a rose.

"Those look great." Cassie stood at her elbow watching her.

"I just hope they taste as good as they look. Everyone seems to think the recipe needs more sugar, but I've added a whole teaspoon to this batch." Lexy set the bag aside and picked up the tray.

"I'll put that in the oven for you," Cassie said, taking the tray from her. "Don't forget to fill out your entry form for the contest tomorrow."

"That's right!" Lexy ran her fingers through her hair. With everything else going on, she'd almost forgotten about the registration. Which reminded her, she needed to visit Violet Switzer. A quick glance at her watch told her that wouldn't happen today—it was almost time for Jack and the *Ladies' Detective Club* to meet her here.

As if reading her mind, the bells on the front door tinkled and she peeked out to see Ruth, Ida and Helen stroll in, their eyes locked on the pastry case like snipers on a target.

"Hey, ladies, where's Nans?" Lexy couldn't hide the disappointment in her voice.

Ruth shrugged. "She said she'd be by later on."

Lexy sighed. "Boy, she sure is taken with this new guy. Has she talked about him to any of you?"

"No," Helen said. "But let her do that in her own time."

"Good advice." Ida rubbed her hands together. "Now, let's get down to business. I'll have an almond scone and a chocolate cream cheese brownie."

Lexy grabbed a large round plate and put Ida's selections on it, then proceeded to pile on the choices from the other ladies, which included lemon squares, scones, brownies and a big piece of German chocolate cake.

Lexy put the plate on one of the cafe tables while the ladies helped themselves to tea at the self-serve station. Then they sat down, spread their napkins out and wrapped half of the pastries inside, then slipped them into their giant, patent-leather purses.

Lexy made herself a dark roast and sat down at the table just as Jack came through the door.

"Good, you guys are already here." He bent and pressed a kiss on the top of Lexy's head then made his way over to the self-serve station for a coffee before pulling a chair up to the table.

"So, tell us this big clue." Ida assessed him with her keen blue eyes.

Jack narrowed his honey-brown ones at her. "You go first."

Ida pinched a corner off her scone and popped it in her mouth as she told Jack how they couldn't come up with anything on Earl prior to nineteen-fifty-five and how Nessbaum seemed clean.

"Of course that could just mean this Nessbaum character hasn't been caught yet," Helen added. "He could still be involved."

Jack nodded and leaned back in his chair. "Right. I found out something interesting about Earl, too. It seems no one missed him after he died. There were no inquiries at the police station—no missing persons reports. Nothing."

Ida narrowed her eyes. "That seems impossible. I mean, surely he had some family."

"From the sounds of it, he was a nasty person," Ruth said. "His family probably disowned him and that's why he moved out here."

"Maybe he even changed his name because he got in trouble back home," Helen suggested.

"And another thing," Jack continued, "he rented that house, and the landlord said she'd get a check like clockwork and then all of a sudden it stopped coming. That's when she went out to the house to collect the rent from him and she realized no one had been there in months, but all his stuff was still there."

"That makes sense—he was dead so he couldn't have packed up his things." Ida reached over to Ruth's plate and broke off a piece of brownie.

"The funny thing is," Jack continued, "she said there were all kinds of holes all over the yard near the fence. She said you couldn't notice them until you inspected closely, which she was very thorough in doing because she wanted to document the damage in case there was any question about her keeping the security deposit."

"Holes? For what?" Lexy asked.

Jack shook his head. "I have no idea. She said they were the size of Mason jars. But no neighbors noticed because there was no dirt mounded up— someone had dug them up and put the dirt back. You had to be standing right on top of them to notice."

"Did she notify the police?" Ruth asked.

"Yep. I read the report. They went out, but didn't find anything amiss. There's nothing about the holes in the report. I guess they didn't notice them, or maybe the landlady made them up so she could keep the deposit."

Ida's eyes sparkled with excitement. "Do you think he buried the money from the insurance scam in those holes?"

Jack shrugged. "Maybe, but if he did, then someone else dug them up."

"The killer!" Helen said over the rim of her teacup.

"Possibly," Jack said. "And there's one more thing. The landlady said there was more damage than the security deposit covered, so she went to the bank the rental checks were drawn on to see if she could contact the person writing those checks. The bank manager said that account had been closed and no forwarding address had been left. When she checked the company name on the check, no such company existed."

"This case is getting very strange," Ida said.

"And it's about to get even more so." Ruth pointed out the window.

Lexy turned to look out the window. Her stomach twisted when she saw what Ruth was pointing at. Watson Davies was making a beeline for Lexy's bakery, and she looked as mad as a cat in a tub full of water.

***

"I knew I would find you all together in here!" Davies stood in front of them, her hands on her hips, looking from one to the other.

"Have you come to arrest one of us?" Ida asked.

"Arrest you? No, I came to join forces with you." She grabbed a chair, jostled Ruth out of the way and pulled the chair up to the table in between Ruth and Helen.

"Now, there's a first," Ida said.

"Not really. I've worked with Mona quite a bit on other cases." Davies looked around the table." Where *is* Mona, anyway?

The ladies and Lexy exchanged a look.

"She had other business to tend to," Ida said primly.

"Really? It's not like her to miss out on a pow-wow about a case. That *is* what you are doing, right?" Davies chewed her bottom lip, then continued without waiting for them to answer. "This isn't good, not good at all."

"Why don't you tell us what's going on," Jack prompted.

Davies sighed and slumped back in her seat. "The Feds have taken over the mummy case."

Jacks brows shot up. "The Feds? What would they want with this case?"

Davies shrugged. "Near as I can figure, they're interested in the insurance scam."

"You know about that?" Lexy asked incredulously. She couldn't believe any of the neighbors had opened up to Davies about it ... unless she'd talked to Johnston—he seemed eager to tell anyone about it.

Davies raised a perfectly plucked brow at her. "Of course I do. I *am* a detective, you know. A *real* detective."

"Well, miss smarty pants," Helen said. "Then you should be able to figure out why the Feds are here."

"It's got to be the insurance ... I know Earl turned up in town under an assumed name. He was probably scamming people in other states and the Feds were tracking him."

Jack made a face. "But that was over fifty years ago. You think they're still interested?"

Davies spread her hands. "They must be. I'm not sure what they are up to, but I know one thing. I'm not going to let them show me up on this one. I intend to find the killer before they do and show them the BRPD is just as good as they are."

"I can't argue with that." Jack tipped his coffee mug toward her. "You want a coffee?"

Davies nodded. Jack went over to the self-serve station and Davies leaned forward, her elbows on the table. "So, I want to join forces. I'll tell you what I know if you tell me what you know."

The ladies looked at each other, then gave each other the secret nod. Then they looked at Jack, who had returned with the coffee.

"Okay, go ahead." Jack waved his hand to indicate his approval and they spent the next twenty minutes bringing Davies up to speed on what they knew, including the receipt Sprinkles had snatched from the basement.

"That's pretty much what I know, too," Davies said once Ida was done. "I didn't know about the receipt. We can't be sure where the dog grabbed that from, but I will go to the pub and see what I can find out. I talked to Nesbaum already. He doesn't know anything. He claims he was refinishing the McDonalds' basement and they called him halfway through and asked him to stop."

"Why would they do that?"

Davies shrugged. "Either he's lying or the McDonalds were involved. I did verify that the McDonalds *were* in Europe that summer, though, so I don't see how *they* could have been the ones to put the body in there."

"Someone else must have done it," Ruth said.

"The stranger," Lexy suggested.

"What if this stranger killed Earl and called Nesbaum pretending to be the McDonalds, then hid the body in the basement and finished it off himself?"

"It seems like the *stranger* would have had to have known an awful lot about what was going on in the neighborhood, then," Jack said. "And how could he have done that without anyone noticing? Surely, one of the neighbors would have seen something going on. The McDonalds must have had someone looking after their place."

Lexy looked down at her half-empty coffee cup, her stomach swooping. Nans always knew what was going on in the neighborhood—wouldn't she have noticed?

"We need to find out more about this stranger," Davies said. "And there's one other thing. The Feds think a woman was involved."

"Why?" Ida asked.

"They found lavender sachets in with the mummy."

"That's right," Lexy said. "I remember seeing them. At first I thought they were potatoes."

Davies gave her a strange look.

"Why would anyone put sachets in there?" Helen asked.

"We figure it was to hide the smell," Davies replied. "A lot of women used them back in the fifties. They put them in their drawers to make their clothes smell nice. Lexy, did your grandmother use lavender sachets?"

Lexy's heart squeezed. *Did* Nans use them? The smell from the mummy room, or at least one of the smells, had been vaguely familiar. Had she recognized the scent of lavender because she remembered Nans clothes smelling like that when she was a little girl?

"I don't think so," Lexy said. Was Davies implying that she thought Nans was involved? Lexy made a mental note to check Nans' drawers next time she was at the apartment just to be sure. "Anyway, the people I talked to said the stranger was a man."

"Yeah, I know." Davies said. "A tall man with bushy blond hair."

"Tall with blond hair?" Lexy screwed up her face and looked at the ceiling trying to remember exactly what Floyd Nichols had told her. "No, I'm pretty sure Floyd Nichols told me he was short with a dark beard."

Davies shook her head. "The McDonalds told me he was tall and blond."

"But they weren't home. They just heard about the stranger from other people," Lexy pointed out. "Maybe they got the description wrong ... not to mention they seem to be a little ... unreliable."

"You've got a point," Davies said. "We'll ask Mona. She was around back then, and with her keen eye for detail, she'll be able to describe him. Not only that, but I bet she can help us straighten this mess out. She's pretty sharp about this stuff. Where did you say she is?"

"Busy," Ida said. "But there's one thing that puzzles me."

"What?"

"Everyone agrees the stranger was a man, right?"

"Right."

"Well, then, if that's the case, he probably didn't load that room up with the sachets, which begs the question ... who was the woman who helped him?"

Chapter Sixteen

Lexy closed the bakery shortly after the meeting. Cassie had baked the meringue cookies to perfection and they sat perfectly lined up on the baking sheet, cooling in the oven. She popped one of the pink confections into her mouth, letting it melt on her tongue.

Did they need more sugar?

She'd eaten so many of them over the past few days, it was impossible to tell. She placed two dozen of them carefully in a white bakery box and headed home ... well, not exactly home. She had made a little bit of a detour to the Sullivans' house, just two houses down from Jack's.

Mary Sullivan answered the door. Intelligent green eyes set wide in a heart-shaped face smiled at Lexy, and Lexy realized Mary was still a beauty even in her late seventies. No wonder Earl had put the moves on her.

"What a surprise. It's nice to see you, Lexy." Despite her words, Mary didn't seem all that surprised.

Lexy held up the box of cookies. "I brought you some cookies from my bakery. It's my new recipe for the Brook Ridge Dessert contest."

"Oh, how nice." Mary took the box from her and gestured for her to come in. "Paddy, look who's here."

Paddy Sullivan appeared in the kitchen doorway, his bald head showing patches of gray on the side.

His face was etched with wrinkles, but his eyes were still bright and intelligent. He smiled at Lexy.

"Hi, Lexy. It's nice of you to stop over." He stepped aside, then pulled out a kitchen chair for Lexy and she sat at the pine plank kitchen table, her lips turning up at the corners in appreciation of the gentlemanly gesture.

"I was just telling Mona we don't see enough of you," Mary said as she bustled around the country-style kitchen, getting a plate and arranging the cookies on it.

"Oh, did you see her recently?"

Mary and Paddy exchanged a look.

"Well, not recently." Mary slid the plate onto the table. "I think we saw her at the senior book sale last month. Right, Paddy?"

"Yes, I think that's the last time we saw her," Paddy said, his focus on transferring the cookies to the smaller plate Mary had put in front of him.

"This was a lovely gesture to bring us your cookies. Do you need feedback on your recipe?" Mary asked.

"I'd love some," Lexy replied. "But actually, I have a question."

"Oh." Mary shot up out of her chair and headed to the stove, then half turned to look at Lexy. "Tea?"

"Yes, thanks."

"So, tell us about this dessert contest." Paddy took a bite of cookie.

"It's the yearly contest, but that's not why I came."

Paddy stopped chewing and looked directly at Lexy, his brows ticking up a fraction of an inch.

"You probably know about the discovery in Jack's basement," Lexy continued.

Mary blanched as she set a dainty porcelain cup with a teabag on a string in front of Lexy. "Yes, terrible to think that was right under our noses"

"Sure is." Paddy reached absently for another cookie, his eyes never leaving Lexy's face.

"You know it was Earl Schute, right?" Lexy asked.

"We heard."

"I know he lived in the neighborhood for a short time. How well did you know him?"

"Hardly at all." Paddy's reply was abrupt. "He lived down on the other street."

"We didn't associate with him," Mary added.

"No? Sam down at the pub said you had a run-in with him more than once."

Lexy pretended to watch the steam curl out of her cup as the Sullivan's exchanged a startled look.

Mary put her dainty, porcelain-white hand over Paddy's larger, work-scarred one. "I guess we should tell her."

Lexy perked up ... now she was getting somewhere!

Paddy nodded. "It's true, we did have a run-in. You see, Earl took a liking to my Mary and I just couldn't have him pressing his amorous intentions on her, so I had to show him what-not."

"My hero." Mary smiled up at Paddy and he returned the look. Lexy could practically feel true love radiating from them and her heart pinched—she sure hoped she wouldn't have to send the lovebirds to jail for murder.

"Just what, exactly, do you mean by 'what not?'" Lexy asked.

"I told him in no uncertain terms to leave her alone." Paddy's face took on a sheepish look. "And maybe I got a little physical, too."

"How physical?" Lexy asked.

"Well, I didn't kill him if that's what you're asking." Paddy avoided Lexy's eyes by digging for another cookie. "He deserved what he got, though."

Mary nodded solemnly in agreement and Lexy decided not to press them. She figured it wouldn't get her anywhere to accuse Paddy, especially not without solid evidence.

"Is it true the McDonalds were on vacation that summer?"

"You mean the summer Earl died?" Paddy asked.

Lexy nodded.

"They were," Mary said. "I remember because Lois sent us a lovely post card. I dug it out after I heard about Earl on the news to check the year. I have it right here."

She twisted around and grabbed a postcard from atop a pine dry-sink behind her, then read the card to Lexy.

"Having a great time. Wish you were here." Lois pointed to the upper right corner. "And there's the postmark right there. August thirteenth, 1955."

Lois handed the postcard over to Lexy. It was a linen-style card, typical of the nineteen-fifties. The image was of a gondola in a crowded canal. Venice. The back was yellowed with a few stains. The message in blue pen had faded over the years, but the postmark was clear as a bell. Lexy handed the card back to Lois, making a mental note to tell Davies about it. That card was proof the McDonalds couldn't have killed Earl.

"And you didn't notice anything strange going on at their house while they were gone?" Lexy asked.

"We can't really see the house from here," Paddy replied. "It's two houses down and offset from us, but we saw the contractor in the driveway. They were having the basement refinished that summer."

"Yeah, I heard," Lexy said. "You know Earl was found stuffed into a small room in the basement. The room had been sealed up as part of the remodel and no one even knew it was there. How do you think he ended up in there?"

Mary and Paddy looked at each other. "We talked about that and we figure it must have been the stranger."

So, they'd seen the mysterious stranger, too, Lexy thought. Something was fishy about this stranger, but she hoped it turned out that the stranger *was* the killer or Bobby Nesbaum, because if not, then Paddy Sullivan and Floyd Nichols were the next most likely candidates.

"Some of the other neighbors reported this stranger, too," Lexy said. "I'm not sure I understand.

Was he just skulking around the neighborhood or was he doing something? Was he here every day? Did you seem him?"

Paddy and Mary glanced at each other out of the corner of their eyes. Mary got busy digging for a cookie in the bakery box.

"He was just seen lurking around. Mostly at night. I can't say as he ever did anything." Paddy pressed his lips together and looked at the ceiling as if trying to dig up his memories of the stranger. "I saw him a couple of times. And once I heard him in the back yard arguing with Earl."

Lexy perked up. "You saw him argue with Earl?"

"Yes, that's right. Least I think it was them. It was dark out and I couldn't really make out who it was or what they were saying, but it was loud. They were out in the back between the backyards and I thought it was odd, since it seemed to be coming from the McDonalds, but I knew they were out of town."

"Really? When was that?" *Could it have been the night Earl was murdered?*

"Oh, I can't remember exactly. I know it was hot, though, as we had the windows open and that's how I heard them."

"Did you happen to see this stranger?"

Paddy and Mary glanced at each other.

"I did catch a glimpse," Paddy said.

"What did he look like?"

The two exchanged another glance.

"I …well …" Paddy stammered.

"He was a ruffian," Mary cut in. "You know the type, all scraggly with facial hair and an unkempt appearance."

"How tall was he? What color hair did he have?"

"He was about average, I'd say with brown hair. Hard to describe, really, wasn't he, dear?" Mary looked at Paddy.

"Yes, he was. Very nondescript," Paddy said.

Lexy felt a niggle of doubt. This was not how the others had described the stranger. Was it possible there was more than one stranger? Or maybe their memories were faulty since all the witnesses were old and over fifty years had passed since they'd seen him.

"Ed Johnston mentioned something about Earl selling insurance." Lexy decided to move on to her next question.

Paddy's face turned red. Lexy noticed he avoided looking at Mary. "Insurance? I don't remember that."

Lexy wasn't surprised. She figured no one wanted to admit to being scammed by Earl.

"So, tell me what you thought of the cookies." Lexy pointed to the bakery box.

"Oh, they were very nice, dear." Mary looked down at her plate, which had a half-finished cookie on it.

"No, really," Lexy said. "You won't hurt my feelings. I've heard the recipe needs more sugar and it's important for me to know, as I want to win. I'm going up against Violet Switzer."

Mary's hand flew to her mouth. "Oh, dear. She's a tough competitor."

"Oh, that's right." Lexy stood to leave. "You probably know her. I heard she used to live in the neighborhood."

"Well, a few streets over," Paddy corrected her.

"Did she know Earl?" Lexy asked.

Paddy and Mary looked at each other again.

Mary shrugged. "I can't rightly say, but if you're going up against her, good luck. She takes her contests very seriously. Maybe a little more sugar in the cookies won't hurt."

They walked Lexy to the living room. As she turned to thank them, a fuchsia sparkle from the table beside the recliner caught her eye. Lexy frowned at the table where a familiar pair of fuchsia-studded glasses was folded up beside the lamp. "Are those my grandmother's reading glasses?"

Mary and Paddy both swiveled their heads to follow her gaze.

"No. No, these are mine." Mary picked them up and shoved them on her face. "They're a very common design for reading glasses. Lots of us ladies have them."

"That's right, and you look lovely in them," Paddy said.

"Well, thanks for coming by and you have a nice day." Mary bumped her shin on the coffee table as she practically pushed Lexy toward the door.

"Thanks. You, too," Lexy said.

"Good luck with the dessert contest," Paddy called out, and then promptly shut the door before Lexy had even stepped off the first step.

***

"I'm beginning to think we should move," Lexy said to Jack over pizza in the kitchen of their home after her visit with the Sullivan's.

"Why is that?"

She glanced out the window. "I think we might be living in a neighborhood of murderers."

Jack chuckled. "Surely, that can't be true. There hasn't been a murder here in over fifty years."

Lexy laughed. "True, and I don't really think any of the neighbors are killers, but I am sure a few of them have been lying to me."

"I remember you were suspicious that Floyd Nichols knew the year Earl died when he claimed he hadn't heard about it on the news." Jack folded a slice of green pepper, onion and hamburger pizza and paused, holding it in front of his mouth. "Did something happen at the Sullivan's?"

"Sort of." Lexy picked a pepperoni off her slice and popped it into her mouth, then wiped her greasy fingers on a napkin. "They're really a sweet couple and you can tell they are devoted to each other. Paddy said he had to defend Mary against Earl. But I think they lied to me, too."

"About Earl being interested in Mary?"

"No, I'm sure that part is true. But I got the feeling something was off. They'd said they hadn't talked to Nans in weeks, but I saw her reading glasses there and I know Nans had those the other day."

"I think you might be reading too much into this. The Sullivan's are old—they probably just lost track of time." Jack reached over and wiped some cheese from the corner of her mouth. "When you're retired, it's harder to remember if it's been a couple of days or a couple of weeks."

"True, but I know Mary lied about the glasses because she said they were hers but she'd just read a postcard to me less than an hour before without any glasses on at all. Why would they lie if they had nothing to hide?"

Jack shrugged. "You tell me.

"There's another strange thing, too." Lexy broke a tiny piece of crust off her pizza and fed it to Sprinkles, who had been sitting next to Lexy and quietly begging for some with pleading, brown eyes. "The descriptions of this stranger everyone seems to have seen are all different."

"Again, that could be due to age and memory. A lot of time has passed. But I have to admit, this case sure is getting strange, especially with the Feds coming in."

Lexy's brows dipped together. "Yeah, what about that? Why do you think the Feds are interested?"

"I don't know. I guess Davies' insurance scam theory makes sense. The two guys they sent, Binder and Fluke, have taken over one of the interrogation rooms down at the station, but they are pretty tight-lipped about what they're doing in there. Davies is all riled up about it."

"I bet she is. Do you think we can trust her?"

"Oh, sure. She's not that bad. She just likes to do things her way and it's better than letting the Feds have total control." Jack grimaced. "From what I've seen, they don't seem too competent and I get the feeling they're more interested in getting the case over with quickly than figuring out what really happened."

Lexy's gut churned, making her wish she hadn't eaten that third piece of pizza. "You don't think they'd just pin it on someone without evaluating the evidence properly, do you?"

"I hope not. But that's why it's important we keep looking into it, too. And that we keep Davies informed so she can do things through proper police channels."

"Okay. I'll call Davies tomorrow and let her in on my conversation with the Sullivan's." Lexy rose from the table, grabbed their plates and put them in the sink. She paused, a fluttery sensation nagging at her stomach as she looked out the window at the yellow crime scene tape stretched across Jack's bulkhead. "You know, I can't help but feel like something isn't right. Like someone is leaving something out or trying to misdirect us."

"I know what you mean. With all the strange 'forgetfulness' going on, I have a bad feeling myself, which is why we need to get to the bottom of this before the Feds do—just in case."

Lexy turned from the window, a puzzled look on her face. "Just in case of what?"

"In case the evidence starts to hit too close to home." Jack's eyes were dark with concern. "Because from where I'm sitting, a lot of the loose ends seem to point directly toward Nans."

Chapter Seventeen

The next morning, Lexy made a surprise visit to Nans. She couldn't shake the feeling that Nans was avoiding her and she didn't want to call ahead and tip her off, lest she make an excuse that she was going out.

She stood in front of Nans' apartment door, her fist raised to knock, her stomach full of the butterflies that had started fluttering after Jack's comment of all the loose ends leading to Nans. He'd said he didn't think Nans was involved, but sometimes evidence can be tricky. He'd pointed out that the Feds didn't know Nans and might interpret things the wrong way. It was best to stick close so they could protect her, if need be.

As Lexy stood there, the door jerked open. Lexy stumbled back.

Nans stared at her from the doorway with wide, startled eyes. "Lexy, you scared the devil out of me. What are you doing lurking around out there?"

"I wasn't lurking. I was just about to knock."

"Oh, did you call? I didn't know you were coming."

"Sorry. I was in the neighborhood and I thought I'd check on you since I haven't seen you in a while." Lexy crossed her fingers behind her back and wondered if she'd be struck by lightning for lying to her grandmother.

Nans eyes narrowed. "Really? It was just the other day we went to Tommy O'Keefe's together."

Lexy hugged Nans and pulled her inside. "Hey, I can come visit my favorite grandma if I want to, right?"

Nans smile warmed her face. "Of course, dear. I was just going down to the clubhouse to see if anyone wanted to play some cards, but that can wait."

"Oh, good, because I was afraid you were avoiding me."

"Avoiding you? Never. I've just been busy. We old ladies have stuff to do, too, you know."

"With your new boyfriend?" Lexy asked slyly.

Nans narrowed her eyes. "Have you been talking to Ida and Ruth?"

Lexy shrugged. "I cannot reveal my sources."

"Well, no worries, there's nothing serious." Nans dismissed the notion with a wave of her hand. "Can I make you some tea or coffee?"

"Coffee would be great." Lexy hung back as Nans started toward the kitchen. "I need to use the bathroom."

"Yes, go ahead, dear. You know where it is."

Lexy sprinted down the hall, a stab of guilt slicing her heart. Instead of turning right into the bathroom, she turned left into Nans' room.

Her pulse pounded as she raced to the bureau, quickly pulling out the top drawer. She stuck her nose in and sniffed. No lavender smell. She stole a quick glance toward the hallway to assure herself Nans wasn't coming and then plunged her hands into the drawer, feeling gently for the telltale bulge.

161

No sachets. She quickly repeated the process for the other drawers then, feeling incredibly relieved at not finding any she darted into the bathroom, flushed the toilet and walked back to the kitchen.

"Having a little trouble this morning, dear?" Nans said handing her a steaming cup full of dark brown brew.

"Huh?" Lexy's heart fluttered, her face flushed. Had Nans seen her rifling the drawers?

"In the bathroom ... seems you were in there a while."

"Oh." Lexy breathed a sigh of relief. Any worries about Nans powers of observation failing in her old age were put to rest—the old lady didn't miss a thing. "I dropped my ring while I was washing my hands."

Nans raised a brow and gestured toward the dining room table, which sat just outside the kitchen. "Have a seat. Tell me about the mummy case. I'm afraid I'm a little out of touch on that."

Lexy brought her up to speed, ending with her visit to the Sullivan's the night before. "Mary and Paddy seem devoted to each other. Did you know Earl was trying to put the moves on her?"

Nans lips pressed together in a thin line. "Yes. Now that you mention it, I remember that. Mary was not in the least bit interested."

"Even so, men have killed for that."

"You're not implying Paddy killed Earl!" Nans voice rose indignantly.

Lexy shrugged. "Have you seen them recently? Talked to them about Earl?"

"No," Nans answered quickly. "Why, it must have been months since I've seen them."

Nans words squeezed Lexy's heart. *Was Nans lying? And if so, what could possibly be the reason?*

"So, tell me about Earl. What kind of neighbor was he?" Lexy asked over the rim of her coffee mug.

"Oh, he was awful." Nans face pinched. "He built that fence in Ed's yard and then he kept his trash all over the back, spilling into our yard. Your grandfather was not happy."

"Did Grampy fight with him?"

"I should say not," Nans bristled. "Your grandfather was a lawman. He didn't agree with having fights in the street."

"But a lot of the other neighbors did," Lexy suggested.

Nans straightened the napkin in her lap primly. "I guess so, I don't really remember exactly."

"Jack said the police talked to his landlady and she said they found holes all over his yard after he disappeared. Did you notice those?"

Nans looked up startled. "Holes? No I never did. To tell you the truth, I never actually looked in his yard ... it was too messy. I always averted my eyes. I didn't even know he was 'missing' really, I just hoped he'd moved out."

Lexy nodded. She could certainly understand that with the way Earl acted. "Did you see this stranger that everyone keeps talking about?"

Nans looked down at the swirly coffee in her cup. "Yes, of course. Well... I saw a shadowy figure in the back yard. Right near the McDonalds' house. I remember being worried because they were in Europe, you know."

"Yes, I know. Which makes me wonder, if they were in Europe, how did someone get the body into their basement?"

Nans' purse chimed, interrupting her from answering. She looked around, spotted the purse in the living room and grabbed it, pulling out her smartphone.

She squinted, then held the phone at arm's-length, heaving a big sigh.

"It's a text, but I can't make out what it says." She handed the phone to Lexy. "Can you read it?"

"Sure." Lexy looked at the screen. "It's Ida. They're on their way over."

"Thanks."

"You're welcome." Lexy handed the phone back. She fidgeted in her chair as she asked the question she didn't really want to hear the answer to. "Why didn't you just pull out your reading glasses, though?"

Nans looked around the room distractedly "I would, but I seem to have misplaced them and, try as I might, I just can't find them in the house anywhere."

***

Lexy didn't have time to tell Nans she knew exactly were the glasses were, because just then the door burst open and Ida, Ruth and Helen bustled in.

"Oh, Lexy, good thing you're here. We wanted to go to Nesbaum's today."

"Don't bother, I already talked to him." A voice boomed from the doorway and they all swiveled to see Watson Davies leaning against the doorframe.

"Did he confess?" Ida asked hopefully.

"Hardly," Davies snorted. "He wasn't very enlightening. I think he was fed up after talking to the Feds. Anyway, naturally he denied being involved and said the McDonalds called and told him to stop working on the basement when he was half finished."

"Really?" Lexy turned to Nans. "Do you think that's true?"

"I ... well ... gosh, that was a long time ago."

Davies came into the room and pushed the door shut. "He showed me the old bill and it reflects him doing only half the job. According to the bill, the last date he was there was August thirteenth—the very day the medical examiner thinks Earl died."

"What? That's strange," Lexy said. "Could he have made that bill up? The mummy case has been in the news and he had to have known you'd be coming to ask sooner or later.

"Possibly," Davies replied. "But I have to say, it does cast suspicion on the McDonalds."

"But they were in Europe," Lexy said. "The Sullivan's have proof!"

"Proof?"

"A postcard from Europe postmarked the day you all say Earl died."

Davies crossed her arms over her chest. "Well, something funny is going on, and I don't know who is involved."

"That's right," Ruth said. "And we intend to get to the bottom of it."

"I don't think you'll get there with Nesbaum."

"You leave that to us." Ida leveled her steely blue eyes on Davies. "We old ladies have ways of making people talk that you police folk can't tap into. He might open up to us more, seeing as we're not officials."

"Well, I guess it can't hurt." Davies walked into Nans kitchen and poured herself a cup of coffee, then turned to regard them over the rim. "Have you guys found out anything new since we last talked?"

Lexy recounted her conversation with the Sullivan's, leaving out the part about Nans' glasses.

"Do you think this Paddy Sullivan character could have killed Earl?" Davies asked Nans.

"No, of course not," Nans answered. "He's no killer, just a man protecting his wife."

"There may be more to this than jealousy or even this supposed insurance scam." Davies turned her baby blues on Nans. "Mona, I haven't had a chance to talk to you about the insurance scam. Did you know anything about it? Your old neighbor, Mr. Johnston, claims Earl had duped a bunch of the neighbors out of money."

"I should say not!" Nans said indignantly. "Mr. Johnston says a lot of things that aren't true. He sits on his porch and makes things up—he's a busybody. I wouldn't put a lot of stock in what he says."

Lexy frowned. "Funny thing, he's the only one who didn't see a stranger that summer. You'd think he would have, being on the porch all the time, but maybe he didn't sit out there back then. Anyway, I suspect Paddy Sullivan knew about the insurance scam ... I got a vibe when I talked to him even though he denied it. I think he didn't want the wife to know he got conned out of the money."

Davies tapped a sparkly blue fingernail on her pursed lips. "Yeah, this insurance scam could be one angle. I think Earl was into something even worse, though. The Feds aren't letting a lot of info out, but I heard from a friend of a friend that someone cut off Earl's big toe."

Nans gasped, her eyes wide. "What? That can't be right."

Ruth said, "Blech, that's gross!"

Helen countered with a simple "Ewww ..."

Ida screwed up her face and looked at Davies. "What? You mean someone cut off his toe and then killed him?"

"Yes, except it was the other way around. Someone killed him and *then* cut off his toe. It was removed post-mortem ... with a pair of curly pinking shears."

Chapter Eighteen

"Who removes a toe with pinking shears?" Ida asked later on when they were in the car on the way to the Nesbaums' house.

Helen scrunched up her face. "You'd have to squeeze really hard to cut through bone with those. It seems impossible."

"I think it could be done with the industrial shears," Ruth said. "It would be similar to using poultry shears to cut chicken bone."

Lexy's stomach churned. "Gross."

"Now, that *is* interesting," Ida pointed out. "Because, the pinking shears point to a woman, just like the sachets."

"But why cut off his toe?" Ruth asked.

"Who knows? Why did someone kill him in the first place? We'll have to wait until we get to the bottom of it and then I'm sure we'll get our answers." Ida poked her head into the front seat. "Got any ideas, Mona?"

Lexy glanced over at the passenger seat where Nans had been silent, apparently deep in thought during the whole trip.

"None at all," Nans said. "It's quite baffling."

"Oh, this is the road right here," Ruth shouted from the backseat, her iPad with MapQuest up on the screen clutched in her hand.

Lexy turned down a side street. The road, although paved, was barely better than a dirt road. It looked like the town had neglected to maintain it for some time and it was pitted with divots and bumps. The ladies lurched in their seats as Lexy drove slowly down it.

"It should be right ... here." Ruth stabbed her finger out the window at an older brick home. A white-haired man was getting into a zephyr station wagon in the driveway.

"That's him!" Ida yelled, ripping the door open and lurching out before Lexy came to a full stop.

"Yoo-hoo!" she yelled as she sprinted across the yard.

The man turned to look at her, his bushy, gray eyebrows drawn over suspicious eyes.

"Are you Bobby Nesbaum?" Ida asked breathlessly.

"Yes." His eyes traveled warily from Ida to the rest of them, who had exited the car and were marching toward him.

"Hi, I'm Ida, and these are my friends." Ida grabbed Lexy's arm and pulled her in front of Nesbaum. "And this poor thing is the woman that owns the McDonalds' old house ... the one they found the mummy in."

Nesbaum's eyes shifted from Ida to Lexy and Lexy saw them soften. "Well, I'm sorry about that. I don't see what that has to do with me, though."

"Oh, I'm sure it doesn't have anything to do with you. We know you didn't have anything to do with it," Ida said slyly. "But you *were* refinishing the basement at the time and I was just wondering if you could help this poor girl. Why, she could lose everything and any little bit of information would be ever so helpful."

Lexy batted her eyelashes and tried to play the part of the maiden in need. She only succeeded in getting an eyelash in her eye, which caused her to have to blink profusely and then poke at her eye to get the lash out.

Nesbaum looked at Lexy with sympathy, but his voice was brisk. "I told the police everything I know."

Ida leaned in and lowered her voice to a conspiratorial whisper. "We don't trust them. Do you? We just want to make sure all bases are covered."

Nesbaum slid his eyes to Lexy again, then sighed and leaned against his car. "I don't think I have anything that will shed any light on the matter. Like I told the police, I only redid half the basement and I sure as heck didn't make any secret room or hide a body in there."

"Which half?" Ruth asked.

"The front and the side walls." Bobby shrugged. "Okay more like three quarters. Anyway, Mrs. McDonald called before I even finished and had me stop work rather abruptly."

"And that was in August of nineteen-fifty-five?" Helen asked.

"Yes. The thirteenth, to be exact. The police made me dig in my records for that date. Luckily, I keep all my invoices."

"That must be a lot of paper." Lexy jammed her finger into her eye to try get it to stop twitching.

Nesbaum straightened with pride. "My basement is pretty full of file cabinets, but I can find what I need quickly. I keep them in chronological order."

"Why, that's very organized of you," Ida said. She knew just how to butter someone up and Lexy could see it was working on Nesbaum. She was actually rather impressed with Ida—normally, Nans did most of the talking, but since Nans had been mostly missing ... or silent ... Ida had taken over the investigation and Lexy noticed she was doing just as well as Nans would have.

"So, I guess you must have known Earl," Ida continued. "The mummy? He hung around *The Elms Pub*, same as you."

To Lexy's disappointment, Nesbaum didn't even flinch at the question. Surely, if he were the killer he would have reacted.

"Yeah, I knew him a little. Didn't like him much." Nesbaum crossed his arms over his chest. "I know how it looks, what with him being found in the wall and it covered up with the same type of plastering I do, but I didn't have any beef with Earl. Even though I thought he was a bum, I didn't kill him."

Ida nodded sympathetically. "Of course not. Do you have any idea who did?"

Nesbaum chuckled. "I wish I did, but I really didn't know him or the McDonalds that well. I mean, I assume they must have had something to do with it, otherwise why would she call me and tell me to stop?"

"Good question." Ruth slid her eyes over to Nans, who was busy inspecting the buds on a pink rose bush.

"I'm not convinced it was the McDonalds, but maybe you can help us find the killer and get the police off your back," Ida said. "Think hard. Do you remember anything or anyone that seemed odd when you were working on the house? A stranger, or maybe something strange Earl did?"

Nesbaum pressed his lips together and cocked his head to the side. "Well, let me think. It was a long time ago, but it does stick out, as it was just so odd for them to make me stop in the middle of working. They said they didn't have the funds to pay me to finish. I didn't notice anything funny other than that ... other than the neighbor who was yelling at Earl."

Ida's brows shot up. "A neighbor was yelling at Earl? Did you tell the police?"

Nesbaum grimaced. "No. I don't really know as it has anything to do with Earl's death. Wouldn't want to get an innocent person in trouble with the police. I didn't want it to look like I was trying to cast suspicion on someone else to take the heat off myself."

"Do you know which neighbor it was and what they were yelling about?" Ida asked.

Nesbaum hesitated a second, then plunged in. "Well, as you can imagine, I was in and out of the house all day, so I saw a lot of goings on in the neighborhood. There was this one neighbor that seemed mighty peeved with Earl. Can't say as I blame him—Earl could really get under your skin. Anyway, I heard them yellin' and screamin' something fierce the last day I was there."

"What about?"

"Well, I couldn't hear everything, but I think it was something about that life insurance Earl was trying to sell to everyone."

"Oh, really?" Ida's white brows shot up. "And who was the neighbor?"

"I don't know the name but he lived right at the end of the street, near the drainage culvert ... thing is, I *thought* I heard one of them say something about how he hadn't heard the last of 'it', but I don't know what happened after that because I never went back."

Ida looked at Nans. "Who lived on the end of the street back then?"

"The end near the culvert?" Nans chewed her bottom lip. "Wel,l I think that was Ron and Esther Witt."

"They still live there!" Lexy said.

Ida's blue eyes sparkled and she turned toward the car. "Come on, girls. It looks like we have another suspect to interrogate."

Chapter Nineteen

"There are too many suspects now. This is getting confusing," Helen complained once they were back in the car.

"Yeah, Mona. Did everyone on the street have a motive to kill Earl?" Ida asked.

"No. Not everyone. These aren't real motives anyway ... just the usual stuff that happens with neighbors who aren't respectful," Nans replied primly. "I mean, no one kills a guy because he puts the moves on your wife or because he keeps a trashy yard."

"Or stole your money?" Helen asked.

"Well, that they do, but not the small amount that I'm sure Earl took for the insurance payments," Nans turned to face Helen, Ruth and Ida in the back seat. "I'm pretty sure we're barking up the wrong tree, talking to my old neighbors. None of them are killers."

"Well, I just wish something would break in this case. It's getting redundant," Ruth pouted.

"I wish they would let us go back into Jack's house," Lexy said as they drove by his house, the yellow crime scene tape still sealing it off.

"Why won't they let you in?" Ida asked. "Aren't they done collecting clues?"

"Who knows? I can only imagine what we'll have to do to fix the mess they left," Lexy answered.

"Not to mention who's going to buy it now that a mummy was found inside," Helen pointed out.

Lexy's stomach felt like a heavy rock had sunk to the bottom of it. Helen had a point. Would no one want to buy Jack's house now? Would they be stuck with it? She didn't want to have to move into Jack's house and sell hers—the one she'd bought from Nans —because it had so many childhood memories. Lexy had images of Jack's house sitting empty and abandoned and her never being able to repay her parents.

As if by universal connection, her cell phone chirped and she glanced down to see it was her mother. The rock in her stomach grew even heavier, but she'd just pulled into the Witts' driveway, so talking to her mother would have to wait.

"I think I'll take the lead on this one," Nans said, and Lexy felt some of her anxiety ease. Finally, Nans was getting back to her old self.

They all jumped out of the car and Nans marched up to the door, which opened even before she knocked.

"Mona! What a surprise!" Ron glanced behind her at the rest of them. "Oh, you brought friends."

"You remember my granddaughter, Lexy." Nans gestured to Lexy, then turned to the other women. "And these are my friends, Ruth, Ida and Helen."

They exchanged greetings and then Nans explained, "We've been looking into the case of the mummy over at the McDonalds' place."

Ron shifted his weight. "Oh, right. I heard about that and I know you have a detective service now. What can I help you with?"

"Well." Nans glanced around the neighborhood uneasily. "We've asked around to all the neighbors that lived here back then about Earl and such. We're just coming to ask you now."

"Oh, well, come on in." Ron pushed the door wide and they all piled into the living room of the small house. It was light and bright inside. White walls, white slip-covered furniture, hardwood floors. Unlike most of the other houses on the street, this one had been nicely redone.

Ron's wife, Esther, bustled out from the kitchen with a tray of fresh-baked lemon squares and tea, making Lexy wonder if they'd been expecting company or if they always kept refreshments on hand.

"Oh, goodie, lemon squares." Ida peered at the tray. "Those are my favorite."

"Take one." Esther gestured to the sofa and chairs. "Everyone, have a seat."

They each took a seat, balancing the lemon squares and coffees precariously on their laps.

"Now, how can we help?" Ron asked.

"The other neighbors have all mentioned the stranger. To tell the truth, I'd forgotten about him. Do you remember that?" Nans asked.

"Oh, yes, quite vividly," Esther answered. "We saw him over by the culvert a few times. Very odd."

Esther gestured out the window and Lexy looked in that direction. The Witts' house was next to a shallow culvert lined with rocks. She remembered from her childhood that it would fill with water, creating a shallow stream when it rained. A smile tugged the corners of her lips with the memory of how she used to like to play there, despite Nan's constant warnings not to.

"And you think he could have been the killer?" Nans' question pulled Lexy's attention back to the room.

Esther and Ron nodded solemnly. "Must have been. Who else would it be?"

"Tell Ron about the witness who saw him fighting with Earl," Ida cut in.

Ron's cheek twitched. He frowned at Ida. "Witness?"

Nans waved her hand dismissively. "Oh, the guy redoing the McDonalds' basement ... what was his name?"

"Nesbaum," Ida supplied around a mouthful of lemon square.

"Yeah, that's right. He says one day he heard you fighting with Earl. Very loudly," Ruth piped in.

"Claims it was the day Earl died," Ida added.

Ron's eyes darted from Nans to Ida. "Well ... I don't ..."

"Oh, I think I remember that," Esther cut in. "I don't know if it was the day he died. I mean, that was over fifty years ago. Who can remember? Anyway, it was about the insurance."

"We heard about that." Helen looked at them over the rim of her coffee cup. "So he tried to sell you insurance, too, then?"

Ron looked down at his hands, clasped tightly in his lap. "We bought it ... and then I found out it was a total scam. I called up the insurance company to check on something and they didn't have any such policy, or even know who Earl was."

"We'd paid a good amount of money for us back then ... two month's' salary," Esther added.

"So you called him out on it." Ruth said it as a statement, rather than a question.

"Yep." Ron straightened in his chair and looked directly at Ruth. "As you can imagine, it made me very angry and I was set on getting my money back."

"And what did he do?" Ida asked.

"He denied it, of course, said it was a mistake and he wasn't going to give me my money back as the policy was real."

Ruth leaned forward in her chair, the coffee sloshing dangerously close the top of her mug. "Then what happened?"

Ron shrugged. "He stormed off. I assumed he went to *The Elms* bar, that's where he usually hung out. I thought he'd be back, but I never saw him again."

"We went to his house to get this so-called proof a couple of times, but he never answered," Esther added eagerly.

Ron grimaced. "I guess we didn't realize he was already dead."

"Did you tell the other neighbors about the scam?" Ida asked.

Ron's face turned red. "No. I didn't know who else had bought a policy ... and ... well, I was embarrassed about getting taken."

"Why would you even buy a policy from someone like him?" Lexy asked. "It sounds like he was a jerk."

"Oh, he acted nice when he first moved in—all businesslike and proper. Then, after a month or so, we saw the real Earl," Esther said. "That's why Ron looked into the policy.

"Is that so?" Helen raised her brows at Nans.

Nans finished chewing her bite of lemon square thoughtfully. "Well, I really don't remember exactly. I didnt have much to do with the man."

"I can see how that would make you mad as a hornet," Ida said to Ron. "But were you made enough to kill him?"

"Of course not!" Ron and Esther both said forcefully.

"Ida, really!" Nans said harshly. "The killer was clearly this stranger."

Ida scrunched her face up at Nans. "But *why* would the stranger want to kill Earl and then *how* did the stranger get into McDonalds' basement?"

Nans, Esther and Ron looked at each other. Nans finally shrugged. "Maybe he had help."

"Could there have been more than one stranger?" Lexy asked, remembering how everyone had described the stranger differently.

"Possibly."

Ida turned to Esther and Ron. "What did this stranger look like?"

Esther and Ron looked at Nans.

Nans said, "I'm not sure. *Shady* would be how I would describe him."

"Was he tall or short?" Ida asked

"Tall."

"Short."

Esther and Ron spoke at the same time, then looked at each other.

"I guess that's subjective," Nans said. "Some might think him tall while others might think him short. See, Ron here is very tall, so if the stranger were shorter than he was, he would describe him as short. Whereas Esther is very short, and she would say he was tall."

"That's right," Esther said. "I guess he was average."

"What color hair?" Ida persisted.

None of them spoke, then Esther ventured, "I think it was dirty blonde."

"That's right. And he wore it medium length," Ron added.

"And he was thin," Esther said.

Lexy and the ladies glanced at each other. The Witts' description didn't really match any of the others. Maybe there *were* two strangers.

"Well, I think we've taken up enough of your time." Nans stood and looked at Ida, Ruth and Helen. "We're done here. Right, girls?"

"I guess ..." Ida stood, glancing down at the Witts uncertainly. "So, you have no idea how Earl ended up dead in the McDonalds' basement?"

They shook their heads. "Sorry, but no."

"I think it's fairly obvious." Nans' voice carried an air of finality. "It was this mysterious stranger. We need to see if we can find out more about him, but I don't feel that it is likely given the time that has passed. I fear the case may never be solved."

"What?" Ida followed Nans out the door. "You're not going to just give up on finding the killer, are you?"

"Oh, no, of course not. We'll keep digging. But not today." Nans stopped and gestured downward toward the chipped red paint on her toes, sticking out from gold, cork-wedged sandal-clad feet. "Today, as you can see, I'm in dire need of a pedicure."

Chapter Twenty

Lexy dropped Nans and the ladies off at the retirement center. As she was pulling out, her phone chirped, reminding her she had a missed call. Her mother.

Lexy hit the callback button, her stomach sinking as the phone rang.

Were her parents calling because of some RV problem?

Lexy did a mental accounting of her bank accounts to try to find some money she'd be able to send them, if need be.

"Lexy, I called you earlier!" Vera's chipper voice blared out of the phone.

"I know. I'm calling you back. I hope everything is okay.

"Yes, dear. We're having a grand old time in the desert."

"You're still in the desert of Maine? Is something wrong with the RV?"

"No … well, yes, but that's not why we're here. We ran into the Schlumbergers—you remember them, don't you? Anyway, we're hanging around with them until Daddy fixes the RV … which is actually why I called."

Lexy's heart pinched. "Do you need money? I have a little bit in savings, but I can sell some investments if—"

"No. No. It's nothing like that," Vera yelled, even louder than usual. "Daddy just needs a part and he says he stored it in Nans' garage. We were hoping you could dig it up and ship it out to us."

Lexy's breath rushed out in relief. "Oh, sure. Whatever you need."

"Okay, it's behind some old boxes in the far right just under the electrical panel. There's a little door there to a small storage section and the doohickey is inside the storage section."

Lexy frowned as she took a U-turn to head back to her house. "Doohickey? Could you be a little more descriptive?"

"Daddy says it's in a blue box with white lettering —Beehive Motors."

"Okay, that sounds easy to find." Lexy hoped.

"Great, then can you Fed-Ex it up to us in care of Desert of Maine Campground, ninety-five Desert Road Freeport Maine, 04032."

"Okay, will do."

"Wait a minute." Lexy heard her mother yelling something in the background, then she came back on. "Gotta go, dear. The horseshoe tournament is starting!"

Vera clicked off just as Lexy pulled into her driveway. She glanced at the time on the phone, then tossed it into the passenger seat.

Just enough time to run in, grab the part, and run to the post office to ship it out before I head off to the Dessert Contest registration, Lexy thought jumping out of her car.

She bent down in front of the detached garage and grabbed the handle for the lift-up door. She yanked and pulled, pushing the door up until it rolled into the ceiling with a squeal of protest. She stood in front of the fully packed space with her hands on her hips, wishing she'd actually made good on the promise to clean it out last spring. As it was, the garage held a variety of things from all three generations. No car, not even one as small as her VW beetle, had fit inside as long as Lexy could remember.

Picking her way through the boxes, old bicycles and paint cans, she headed toward the back corner, scanning the wall for the storage area. She found it behind a stack of boxes. The storage area was only a crawl space. The door was about three feet off the ground. Lexy pushed the boxes off to one side and crouched down in front of the door, which was a thin slab of wood, secured with a metal hook-and-eye latch. She opened it, brushing cobwebs out of the opening. The smell of old, dry wood tickled her nose as she peered into the darkness.

Lexy felt a chill run up her spine as she got a feeling of deja-vu. The scene reminded her of just a few days earlier when she had knelt in front of the hole in Jack's basement and peered into the secret room at the mummy. Hopefully, she wouldn't find a dead body in here today.

Lexy blinked into the dark space. Just inside the door were an old helmet, a basketball, and what was left of a croquet set. She shoved them out into the narrow aisle she'd made on her way in, then got on her hands and knees and pushed her upper body inside. She could see a little better now, and thought she spotted a light blue box with white writing over on the right. She twisted her torso, reaching out her right hand to grab it.

She grabbed the edge of the box, but it was stuck. She tugged. It didn't budge. She hoisted herself in a little further. The box appeared to be wedged between some two-by-fours that made up the framing of the storage space—something else was keeping it wedged in. She shoved her hand into the space beside the box and pulled.

The box popped out and along with it, a red flip-flop.

Something niggled at Lexy's memory. Where had she seen a red flip-flop before?

Then it hit her, turning the blood in her veins to ice. She knew where she'd seen one ... Earl's mummy had been wearing a red flip-flop and she hadn't seen another one in the secret room. She thought back ... what foot had it been on? Picturing the mummy lying there, she remembered—it was the right foot. She looked down at the flip-flop in front of her and a jolt of panic shot through her—the flip-flop was for a left foot.

Was this the other flip-flip that Earl had been wearing when he died? And, if so, what in the world was it doing hidden in Nans' garage?

***

Lexy stared at the red flip-flop lying on floor in front of her, just inside the small storage room. It was probably a coincidence. Surely, Earl wasn't the only one to wear red flip-flops, and just because he appeared to have lost one and there was only one here in Nans' garage didn't really mean anything. It was circumstantial.

Lexy wondered if the FBI had advanced tests they could do to prove this flip-flop was the mate to Earls, and if so—

"Are you trying to hide from me?"

Lexy whirled around to see Watson Davies standing just inside the garage door.

"What? No!" Lexy sprang up from her position on the ground, kicking the small storage room door shut as she did. "What are you doing here?"

Davies surveyed her, an amused look on her face. "I was driving by and saw your car. I thought I'd swing in so we could catch up."

"Driving by?"

"Yeah, on my way to Jack's to give it one last go-through before we clear the crime scene."

"Oh." Lexy relaxed and blew a stray lock of hair off her forehead. "I was just in here looking for a part for my parent's' RV."

It wasn't a lie ... just not the whole truth.

Davies looked around. "You have a lot of stuff in here."

"Yep." Lexy glanced behind her at the door to make sure it was closed. "Some of it is left over from when Nans moved to the retirement home and my parents sold their house and decided to travel the country."

"It's like a time capsule." Davies leaned over and looked in one of the boxes, causing Lexy's heart to leap. The last thing she needed was for Davies to start rummaging around and find the flip-flop ... or something else Nans might have stored in here.

Lexy picked her way back toward the front of the garage. "It's hot in here and there are spiders. Let's talk outside."

"I wanted to ask if you guys got anything out of Nesbaum." Davies glanced backward over her shoulder as Lexy pushed her out into the driveway.

Lexy brushed the dirt and cobwebs from her shirt. She considered holding back about Ron Witt, mostly out of habit. She wasn't used to sharing information with Davies, but they were on the same team now and she might need Davies help in the future.

"As a matter of fact, we did," Lexy said.

"Well, those sneaky old ladies." Davies face lit in an appreciative smile. "What did you find out?"

Lexy told her how Nesbaum had heard Ron Witt fighting with Earl and their subsequent trip to talk to Ron and Esther.

Davies chewed on a sparkly blue fingernail. "Do you think this Ron guy could have done it?"

"I don't know. He admitted being mad and embarrassed about it, but people don't just go around killing someone because they are mad." Lexy twisted her mouth in thought. "I really don't think he did it. It would be out of character."

"What about the other neighbors? They had motives, too," Davies pointed out.

Lexy pictured the red flip-flop in the storage room and her stomach sank. "They did, but not strong enough motives to justify murder. Besides, I can't imagine anyone in the neighborhood doing it."

"But it's got to be tied to the neighborhood. He was found in the McDonalds' basement and there's no way a stranger would have known to put him in there."

She had a point. Only the neighbors would have known about the basement remodel, unless the stranger had noticed Nesbaum coming and going, or had found out some other way.

"What about *The Elms Pub*?" Lexy suggested. "We know Earl hung around there and the receipt I found from Sprinkles might have been from him. Maybe it was someone he had a run-in with there and they also knew about the McDonalds' basement renovation, because Nesbaum hung there and he might have mentioned it."

"We don't know if that receipt was in the sealed-off room with Earl," Davies cautioned, "though your dog *did* run in there, so it's possible. Or she could have gotten it from the mess in that basement which would be another clue tying the McDonalds to Earl."

"Well, that doesn't seem like much of a clue. I mean, lots of people went to the bar and we already have proof the McDonalds were in Europe."

"True. But I talked to Sam down at the bar, and he didn't know of anyone who might have wanted to kill Earl. And anyway, it doesn't make sense, because if it was someone from the bar, then how did they get the McDonalds to call off Nesbaum?"

"Maybe they didn't. Nesbaum could have been in on it and doctored his receipts, just in case someone came asking."

"Maybe Nesbaum and this stranger were in on it together."

"That's another thing that bugs me. Everyone is describing the stranger differently. I was wondering if there could be more than one."

"Maybe." Davies shook her head. "But what was their motive? And why were they hanging around the neighborhood? It doesn't make much sense. If some murdering strangers wanted Earl, they'd just go get him, not skulk around people's backyards, like the neighbors are describing."

"I know. Nothing makes sense." Lexy sighed. "And what's the deal with his toe being cut off?"

Davies worried her bottom lip. "I don't know, but it points to something deeper than neighborly feuds."

"Right." Lexy's hopes soared. Of course, Davies must be right. There was something else going on they hadn't yet uncovered, and it had nothing to do with her neighbors—or Nans—being killers.

"Too bad the Feds don't seem to think so."

Lexy's hopes took a nosedive. "Oh, no?"

"No. Near as I can tell, they haven't looked into much else other than the neighbors, and it seems like they are close to coming to a conclusion."

"A conclusion? You mean they think they know who the killer is?"

"It seems that way. And I don't have a warm-fuzzy feeling they are on the right track. Unfortunately, I fear we're racing the clock here, now, and we need to step up our game and come up with some concrete evidence, fast." Davies expression turned grim. "Otherwise, I'm afraid the Feds are getting ready to put the cuffs on an innocent person just to stamp the case closed."

Chapter Twenty-One

Lexy felt a tightness in her chest as she watched Davies drive off. Would the Feds really make a hasty arrest just because they wanted to close the case and clear out? And who would it be—one of her neighbors? Or worse—her own grandmother?

Glancing uneasily at the storage area in the back of the garage, she wondered if Nans had been involved in Earl's death. If not, why did she have his shoe?

Nans was going to have some explaining to do.

But first, Lexy needed to get that RV part. She crouched down and opened the door to the small storage space again, her gaze falling on the red flip-flop. Guilt lapped at her stomach—she probably should have told Davies about it, but couldn't bring herself to incriminate her own grandmother.

She quickly shoved the flip-flop back into the hiding place behind the two-by-four, pulled the RV part out and closed the door. Then she shoved the boxes back in front of it, just in case. It wouldn't do to have someone else go snooping around in there and find it.

After addressing the box to her parents at the Desert of Maine, she hopped into the car. The phone she'd tossed onto the passenger seat earlier caught her eye. It was time to call Nans.

Lexy dialed and waited for Nans to answer. And waited. And waited.

"Dang it!" Nans wasn't answering. Lexy had a good mind to hunt her down and find out about the shoe in person, but she didn't have time. She'd have to hurry if she wanted to get the RV part to the post office and make it to the town hall in time to fill out the final registration forms for the Brook Ridge Dessert contest.

She'd already neglected her business too much this week and she couldn't miss out on the contest. Which reminded her, there were quite a few things at the bakery that needed her attention, not the least of which was finalizing the meringue recipe. She couldn't let investigating Earl's death cause her business to fall by the wayside.

She raced to the post office, mailed the part and then headed to the town hall two streets over. As she pulled in, a familiar red Mustang sat in the lot—Violet Switzer.

Lexy got out of her car and marched into the town hall. She wasn't about to let a little old lady in a hot rod intimidate her. She pulled the heavy oak and brass doors open and peered inside, expecting to see the tiny, white-haired tornado lying in wait for her. But, to her surprise, Violet was nowhere to be seen.

Lexy stepped onto the white and tan marble floor of the foyer, marched up to the window and looked through the glass at the clerk, Penny Mayfair, who was seated on the other side.

"I'd like to register for the Desert Contest," Lexy said.

Penny glanced up at her over the rims of her glasses.

"Oh, hi, Lexy ... now, let me see." She shuffled some papers around on her desk, then frowned. "I think they're over there."

She pushed herself up out of the chair and shuffled over to a tan-colored metal filing cabinet where she proceeded to open the drawers and slowly thumb through the files.

Lexy tapped her fingernail on the counter while she waited, her checkbook lying open in front of her. It seemed to be taking an awfully long time, and Lexy was lulled into a daze when—

"Don't know why you're bothering."

Lexy's heart leaped at the voice in her ear and she spun around, then looked down to see Violet Switzer sneering up at her, the dessert contest forms clutched in her hand.

"Hello, Violet," Lexy said cooly. "I disagree. In fact, I think I have the winning recipe."

"Don't think so, I've tasted your cookies." Violet made an exaggerated pucker-face that accentuated her cross-etched wrinkles. "They're a bit tart, if you ask me."

Lexy frowned, remembering the box of cookies Violet had left on her doorstep. "How did you get my cookies, anyway?"

"Oh, I have my ways." Violet shoved her aside, then pushed the papers over to Penny. "Here's my entry, dear. Now, don't forget, I want placement in the front center of the table."

Lexy's mouth fell open as she watched Violet slide a twenty-dollar bill across the counter. Penny grabbed the bill and tucked it into her pocket.

"You can't do that!" Lexy sputtered. Everyone knew the front center spot on the table where they placed the dessert entries was the most prestigious spot. Lexy had been told the locations were chosen by picking the name out of a hat. She stared at Penny, who just shrugged.

Lexy turned to Violet to give her a piece of her mind, but her brain seized up. Her mouth hung open and no words came out. The woman had a way of jumbling Lexy's thoughts.

Violet sneered up at her and clomped off, the rubber soles of her orthopedic shoes squeaking as she walked toward the exit.

Lexy turned back to Penny. "Did she just buy the best spot?"

"What?" Penny's brows dipped and she stared hard at Lexy. "Certainly not! I have no idea what you are talking about. Here's your forms."

Lexy swiveled her head around to stare at the door as it shut behind Violet, then grabbed the forms from Penny. She'd let Violet get to her again, but that was going to stop right now. She shoved the forms into her purse and sprinted toward the door.

***

Lexy burst out of the door in time to see the Mustang's tail lights take a right turn out of the lot. She jumped into her VW Beetle and squealed after Violet in pursuit.

I'll show Violet Switzer that she's not the only one who can follow people around and try to intimidate them!

Lexy followed the Mustang as it wound its way through town, careful to keep a few cars behind her so Violet wouldn't know she was being tailed. She wasn't exactly sure what she was going to do, but she knew it was smart to keep the element of surprise on her side.

Lexy could hardly keep the smile from her face as she pictured the startled look on Violet's face when she snuck up on her. Hopefully, it would throw her off-kilter, just like Violet had been doing to Lexy.

Violet pulled into the library parking lot and Lexy circled the block, then pulled in in time to see Violet disappear through the library's large front door. Lexy whipped into a parking spot and sprinted up the steps, pulling the door open slowly and slithering in behind one of the columns in the foyer.

Peeking out from behind the column, she scanned the room for Violet. She wasn't in the main room. Lexy stepped further into the room, just in time to see the top of Violet's white-haired head disappearing down the stairs. Lexy wondered if that was where they kept the books on intimidating competitors.

She crossed over to the stairs slowly to give Violet enough time to get down them before she descended.

Lexy hadn't been down here in ages and the first thing she noticed was how quiet it was. The carpet and rows of books muted any sound. The second thing she noticed was that it was set up like a maze, with bookshelves shooting off in all directions. How would she ever find Violet in here?

She started down the main aisle, going slowly and trying not to make any noise as she looked from left to right down the side aisles. They were all empty, which seemed impossible. Violet had to be down here somewhere.

And then she heard the hushed tones of whispering voices.

Lexy stopped, cocking her ear in the direction of the voices. They were coming from just up ahead. She crept forward silently, until it sounded like they were in the next aisle. Inching her way to the end of the row, she peered around the corner.

Violet stood in the aisle, pretending to look at a book. From where Lexy stood, she could see the arm of another woman, also pretending to read a book. It was obvious the two were having some sort of secret conversation.

Why would Violet be having a clandestine meeting in the library?

Lexy wondered if it had something to do with the dessert contest. Violet had paid off the town clerk. Maybe she was secretly meeting with one of the judges to bribe—or blackmail—them to vote in her favor. From what Lexy knew of Violet, she wouldn't put either past her.

Lexy inched forward ... if she could just get a look at the other person or hear what they were saying, it might give her some ammunition with which to fight Violet. She craned her neck, stretching to see the other woman.

Finally, she caught a glimpse. It was only a partial view of the other woman's face because she was holding the book up to cover her, but it was enough to set Lexy's heart pounding. She pulled her head back, gasping in a breath.

The other woman was Nans.

***

Lexy turned and ran down the aisle toward the stairs. A book fell from the shelf in her wake, clattering to the floor. As she sprinted up the steps, she heard Violet's startled voice echoing below.

"Who's there?"

Lexy didn't answer. She turned at the top of the stairs and, ignoring the librarian's disapproving look, made a beeline for the parking lot.

Lexy's stomach churned. Why would Nans be meeting with Violet? Surely, it couldn't have anything to do with the dessert contest—as far as she knew, Nans was not involved. But the only other thing she could think of that they had in common was Earl Schute.

With her head spinning, Lexy pulled out of the library parking lot. She didn't know what to think. Nans' oddly disinterested behavior, her lying about talking to the Sullivans, the red flip-flop and, now, this secret meeting, gave Lexy a very bad feeling.

She didn't know what was going on with Nans, and she didn't have much time to figure it out. She pointed the car in the direction of the best people she knew who could help her—Ruth, Ida and Helen.

Chapter Twenty-Two

Lexy found Ruth, Ida and Helen clustered around their usual table in the lobby of the Brook Ridge Retirement Center. The three women looked to be in a heated conversation and, even though Lexy was bursting with the information about Nans, she didn't dare interrupt.

"My money is on Nesbaum ... he had means and opportunity," Ida said.

"But what's his motive?" Ruth asked.

"I bet we could dig one up," Ida replied.

"Nope, I bet you a twenty it was that Paddy Sullivan." Helen's eyes took on a dreamy look. "A man protecting his lady. It's so romantic, and jealousy is one of the prime motives for murder."

"Pshaw," Ruth cut in. "I raise your twenty to thirty. I think it was that couple, Esther and Ron Witt. He got taken in by Earl's scam and that's reason for killing, in a lot of men's eyes."

"What about the stranger?" Ida asked.

"He probably helped," Helen answered. "He fits in here, somehow. I'm just not sure exactly how."

Ruth scrunched up her face. "But don't you find it suspicious that they all describe him differently?"

"Maybe they are covering up for him," Helen suggested.

"But how would the neighbors even know this stranger?" Ruth asked. "How would they have gotten hooked up with him?"

"I don't know. There seems to still be some missing pieces." Ida turned to Lexy. "What do you think?"

That was the problem. Lexy didn't know *what* she thought. Should she tell them about the flip-flop and the meeting with Violet? She knew Nans couldn't possibly have been involved with a murder, so there must be a logical explanation and she knew the ladies would help her find it.

"I don't know what to think about who did it, but I have—"

"It doesn't matter what you guys think," Davies cut in from across the lobby. "The Feds have some evidence and I'm afraid it implicates Mona."

"What?" Lexy's heart twisted.

Davies crossed the room and stood in front of the table. "I hate to tell you, but they said they looked at the old phone records and Mona made a late-night call to the McDonalds in Europe ... on the night Earl died."

"So? Maybe she was calling them late so it would be convenient in the time zone the McDonalds were in," Lexy suggested.

"Maybe, but they also looked into her bank records and it turns out she wrote a check to Earl for two thousand dollars." Davies shrugged. "And with the lavender sachets being in with the body, the Feds are looking for a woman."

"Dang," Ida said. "That doesn't look good, especially since she told us she didn't know about the insurance scam."

And that's not even the worst of it, Lexy thought, the image of the red flip-flop coming to mind.

"You don't think Mona's involved, do you?" Ruth asked Davies.

"Murder?" Davies shook her head. "Nah. Mona's not the type. But the Feds don't know her like we do. That's why we have to act fast and figure out who did it so we can present them with the evidence."

"And just how do you propose we do that?" Ida asked.

"We already have a bunch of suspects." Davies held up five fingers pointing to each one as she ticked off the suspects. "We have Nesbaum who refinished the basement, we have Nichols who fought with Earl over their yard, we have Sullivan whose wife Earl harassed, and we have Ron Witt, who fought with him over the insurance scam."

"And the stranger," Ida added.

"Right, whom they've all been describing differently," Davies reminded them.

"That's great, but how do we narrow it down?" Helen's voice was pitched with a hint of exasperation.

Davies looked ruefully at the three women. "I've come up with a plan, but I'm afraid I can't include the three of you."

"What?" Helen scowled at Davies.

"Well, I never!" Ida said.

"Why not?" Ruth asked.

"The way I see it, we have to get them all together in the same room and force the truth out of them. I need to make it seem official and it's not going to look that way with the three of you hovering around." Davies' face softened. "Sorry. I promise we'll let you know exactly what happens."

"Well, what do you plan to do, exactly?" Ida asked.

"I'm going to bring them down to the interrogation room. I've arranged it so it will seem official, but it's all off the books, so to speak," Davies said. "The Feds don't know about it so we'll be able to act on the information ourselves first. I suspect someone is lying. Once the truth comes out, we'll be able to figure out what really happened and capture the real killer *before* the Feds pin it on Mona."

***

Davies promised to contact all the suspects and arrange the meeting for later that night. The ladies took their bruised ego's to their respective apartments and Lexy retreated to her car in the parking lot.

She felt sick thinking about how the Feds could blame the murder on Nans. But, she had to admit, there was a lot of incriminating evidence stacked up against her grandmother ... and some of it the Feds didn't even know about. Like how she'd lied about visiting the Sullivan's and how she had a red flip-flop in her garage. Not to mention how Nans had claimed not to know Earl and then backtracked. And now, the fact that she'd called the McDonalds that night and been scammed by Earl.

But Nans couldn't be involved. Lexy wouldn't believe it. Her grandmother spent her time catching criminals ... she couldn't be one. And if it turned out she was involved, Lexy was sure she would have a darned good reason. In fact, she should just come right out and ask her.

Lexy rummaged through the purse on her lap for the phone, then dialed Nans. Of course, she didn't answer.

"Arggh!" Lexy shoved the phone in her purse and tossed it in the passenger seat in exasperation. It tipped, spilling out the forms for the dessert contest.

I guess I might as well fill these out, Lexy thought. She still had to take care of business, even if Nans was about to be arrested for murder.

While filing out the forms, her thoughts turned to Violet. Lexy wondered what else the woman had done to secure a first place prize. And why had she been meeting with Nans? Did it have something to do with Earl Schute? Lexy remembered that Violet lived in the neighborhood back then and Sam had said she'd asked about Earl at the pub. Maybe it would be a good idea to pay a visit to Violet. At the very least, Lexy could scare up more information on the contest and how Violet intended to win it.

Glancing at her watch, she saw she had just enough time before she had to get to Davies' meeting, so she started her car and pointed it toward Chapel Hill.

***

Lexy didn't know what she was expecting Violet's house to look like. She had pictured something dark and gloomy—a dilapidated mansion with turrets and spikes that loomed above her, broken shutters flapping in the breeze. But the house at thirty-three Chapel Hill Drive was exactly the opposite. A neatly trimmed, brick Cape Cod with a white picket fence and lush, colorful gardens. Lexy might not have believed it was Violet's house if it weren't for the red Mustang in the driveway.

She made her way slowly up the brick path to the side porch, her heartbeat picking up speed as she got closer to the door. The backyard was filled with several types of purple flowers. The welcoming porch was decorated with rustic birdhouses and colorful, Chippy-paint tables. Two rockers sat empty, but Lexy could tell they were often used. The house exuded charm in stark contrast to its owner.

Lexy squared her shoulders, stepped up to the door and knocked.

There was movement behind the starched, white eyelet curtains in the window and Violet's face peered out, then the door whipped open. Violet stood in the doorway, scowling at her.

"What are *you* doing here?"

Lexy's gaze drifted over Violet's head into the gleaming blue and white kitchen. Mixing bowls, measuring cups and various baking ingredients sat out on the counter, but otherwise, the kitchen was neat as a pin. The pungent smell of lemon tickled Lexy's nose.

"Hi, Violet" Lexy tried to smile at the formidable woman. "I thought maybe we could be friends. You know, talk about the dessert contest and maybe you could tell me how you know my grandmother."

Lexy saw something flash in Violets eye for a second. "What makes you think I know your grandmother?"

"Well, you lived in that neighborhood, right? The one Earl Schute was killed in." Lexy tried to shake the woman up, but Violet didn't flinch. She was staunch as a redwood tree.

"Yep. So? You think just because I lived near your grandma that we're gonna be friends?"

"Well, I was kind of hoping that—"

Slam!

Lexy stood, staring open-mouthed at the door that Violet had just slammed in her face.

"Hey, you can't just slam the door on me," Lexy yelled, bending over to peer through the crack in the curtains. Inside, Violet made an unlady-like gesture and jerked the curtains closed.

Lexy raised her tightly balled fist to knock again and then realized it wasn't worth the trouble. She could hear the phone ringing inside as she turned away.

I'll show her. I'll win that damn contest if it's the last thing I do!

As Lexy stormed toward the steps, a breeze from the west wisped across her heated cheeks bringing a delicious floral scent with it.

Lexy stopped. Something niggled at her memory. Where did she know that scent from?

Her heart skipped a beat. The scent was lavender —the same scent that had been in that secret room with Earl.

She jerked her head toward the garden to get a better look at the plants. The medium-sized ones she recognized as wolfsbane, the smaller ones on the edge were pansies, but those tall ones, she wasn't familiar with. They must be lavender.

Violet grew her own lavender—that had to be one heck of a coincidence.

She couldn't wait to tell Davies, but as she started down the steps, her gaze fell on one of the tables next to the rocker. She hadn't noticed before, but at this angle, she could see the drawer was open ... and something was inside. She tiptoed over and slowly slid the drawer out to get a better look.

Her heart jerked in her chest and she sucked in a ragged breath when she saw what it was.

A lavender sachet.

Chapter Twenty-Three

Lexy ran for her car and dove for the cellphone. She tried Davies first. No answer. Then she tried Nans. No answer. Then she tried Ida, Ruth, Helen and Jack—none of them answered.

Where was everyone?

She drove away from Violet's, bursting at the seams to tell *someone* about the lavender sachets. Violet had lived in the neighborhood when Earl was murdered. Violet had been asking about Earl in the pub.

Could Violet be the killer?

But, if she was, then why did Nans have the red flip-flop and why did the two of them have a secret meeting?

The thought that Nans and Violet could have been in on it together flitted through Lexy's mind, but she didn't want to believe it. She wondered if she should refrain from telling Davies about the sachets. No, if Nans was involved it was innocently. Maybe Violet had something on Nans and was forcing her to keep the secret.

Bam!

Lexy had been so deep in thought that she hadn't seen the pothole in the road. She cringed at the *clunk-clunk-clunk* sound that followed.

It sounded like she had a flat tire.

Lexy stopped and got out and, sure enough, it was flat.

"Damn it! Why now?" Lexy kicked the tire and then reached in the window for her cell phone to call roadside assistance. She leaned against the car to wait in frustration while she wore out her cellphone, trying to get a hold of anyone to tell them about the sachets.

To add insult to injury, just as they were putting the spare tire on, Violet's red Mustang roared by. Lexy thought she saw Violet sneering at her out the window, but she couldn't be sure.

Finally, the tire was changed and Lexy sped off to the meeting with the spare on—she didn't have time to stop at the gas station. She was late for the meeting!

Lexy ran into the station and burst into the room Davies had secretly procured for the meeting.

A sea of faces looked up at her from the table. Lexy was shocked to see one of those faces belonged to Violet Switzer.

Lexy narrowed her eyes at Davies and pointed at Violet. "What's she doing here?"

"Violet lived on the street and had contact with Earl, so I asked her to come," Davies answered. "But everyone here claims they don't know a thing about Earl and they keep insisting it was some stranger. I was just about to impress upon them how serious this is and how the evidence is quickly stacking up against Nans."

Lexy's stomach twisted at the sight of Nans' pale face. She just *knew* that Nans did not kill Earl Schute.

"It wasn't Nans. It was Violet—she has lavender sachets!" Lexy blurted out.

Violet's eyes grew wide.

Nans stood up. "Now, see here, that doesn't mean a thing."

Why was Nans sticking up for Violet? Lexy wondered. Judging by the perplexed look in Violet's eyes as she looked up at Nans, she was wondering the same thing.

Lexy addressed Nans. "No, but at least it's a clue that points to someone besides you. I know you didn't kill anyone."

"Well, I don't think any of us here is a cold-blooded killer," Nans said evasively.

Davies tried to rein the meeting in. "Hold it. Let's just stick to the program. I need you all to tell me what happened that summer or I'm afraid the Feds are going to lock Mona up."

"And Violet," Lexy added hopefully.

Paddy Sullivan slammed his hand on the table and pushed himself up. "Now, wait just a minute. I'm not letting Mona or Violet go to jail for something I did. This pretense has gone on long enough and it's time to put a stop to it. I'm the one that did it. *I* killed Earl Schute."

Lexy's mouth fell open and she noticed Nans' jaw tighten.

Violets eyes softened as she regarded Paddy. "Now, Paddy, you don't have to—"

"Are you confessing?" Davies cut in. "Do you realize this means you'll go to jail? You had better be sure you really did this and aren't just covering for someone."

Paddy glanced down at Mary. She nodded up at him, her eyes shiny with tears.

"No. I did it," he said. "You see, he came along the street drunk as usual and started trying to make time with Mary, and I'm afraid I let my temper get away from me and whacked him with a baseball bat in the head."

Mary put her hand over Paddy's and looked up at him adoringly. "My hero."

"Wait a minute!" Floyd Nichols shouted. "You didn't kill him, I did and I'm not about to let you take the blame for it!"

Everyone's heads whipped around to stare at Nichols on the other end of the table.

"Now, Floyd, you don't need to try to cover for me," Paddy said.

Nichols gave Paddy a confused look. "I'm not covering for you. I really did kill him. He came stumbling over to my yard and nearly took down my fence. I was fed up, so I punched him right in the face and he fell down like a baby. It didn't take much, really. I was surprised because he kind of fell right into it. I think he was drunk."

"You killed him with a punch?" Davies asked incredulously.

Floyd shrugged. "I guess so. He went down and then I checked him and he wasn't breathing."

Ron Witt shot up from his seat, looking confused. "No. No. No. It wasn't either of you. I killed Earl! I clubbed him and he drowned in the culvert!"

"Wait a minute!" Davies stood up. "You can't all have killed him. Are you guys covering for each other?"

Paddy, Floyd and Ron looked at each other in confusion.

"No. I swear," Paddy said.

"Nope, I did it. He fell like a log right in the backyard next to the McDonalds," Floyd added.

"He was face down in the water," Ron said. "I'm sure I killed him."

Davies slid her eyes over to Nans and Nans shrugged.

"I didn't see any of it," Nans admitted.

Davies narrowed her eyes. "But you *did* see Earl that night?"

"Not alive."

"Okay, okay. Let's back up a minute, here." Jack, who had been listening quietly, piped up from the end of the table. "It seems you all admit to seeing Earl that night. Now, let's go over the events and see if we can figure out what really happened."

"Good idea," Davies said. "Paddy, you go first."

Paddy pressed his lips together. "Well, some details are fuzzy, but near as I can recall, Mary and I were out in the backyard looking at the stars when we saw Earl walking through the yards towards us."

"What time was that?" Jack asked.

Paddy looked at Mary and they both shrugged. "I don't know—long after supper time. Like I said, it was dark."

"I remember it was after Wheel of Fortune, so maybe ten o'clock?" Mary offered. "And Earl must have been at the bar because he was acting all cocky and belligerent."

"Anyway," Paddy continued. "He came swaggering up and started hitting on Mary, right in front of me! I tried to get him to leave but he wouldn't and when he tried to get physical with Mary ... well, I just got mad and picked up the nearest thing and clobbered him."

"And that was a baseball bat?" Davies asked.

"Yep."

"You wouldn't happen to still have it, would you?"

Paddy's expression turned sheepish. "No, I got rid of it darn quick."

"Okay," Jack continued. "So you hit him with a bat and then you dragged him to the McDonalds' basement?"

Paddy glanced at Nans, who nodded.

"No ... well, not right away." Paddy tilted his head toward Nans. "I panicked and called Mona. She always knows what to do."

Everyone turned to Nans, who simply shrugged.

Jacks left brow ticked up. "And what did *you* do, Mona?"

"Well, the way I see it, Paddy did everyone a favor and I just wanted to help him out. No one liked

Earl and Paddy got rid of him for us. I knew Paddy was no murderer that needed to be prosecuted. So, I came up with a plan. I told him to get a trowel and some tools and meet me in the back yard. Then, I called Ron Witt, Floyd Nichols and the McDonalds."

"So your neighbor killed someone and you called the other neighbors to help you cover it up?" Davies asked Nans.

Nans nodded. "Things were different back then. Neighbors stuck together. Plus, we all had big problems with Earl and we were a tight bunch back then. I knew they would help."

Lexy glanced around the table to see all the neighbors nodding in agreement.

Ron narrowed his eyes at Nans. "Wait a minute. Did you say you called me that night?"

"Yes, of course. I gave the usual signal—two-and-a-half rings. I thought that's why you called back."

"No, I didn't even know you called. I was calling *you* to help me get rid of Earl."

Nans give him a puzzled look. "Oh, gosh, I was in a bit of a tizzy. It's not every day you have to come up with a plan to hide a body. I didn't hear you say you thought you killed Earl, I thought you said *Paddy* killed Earl!"

"Well, I killed him after Paddy did, so I don't see how Paddy could be the real killer."

"I do," Jack cut in. "Maybe Earl wasn't actually dead. Maybe he just passed out after Paddy hit him."

"And he got up and came to my place?" Ron asked.

214

"It's possible," Jack replied.

"But wouldn't Paddy, Mary or Nans have seen him get up?" Davies asked.

Nans shook her head. "I was busy calling people and getting stuff together ... why it took a good half-hour, I think, before I went outside after Paddy's call."

"Us, too," Paddy and Mary chorused.

"So it's possible he wasn't quite dead." Jack tapped his finger on his lips. "How did you determine he was dead?"

"Well, he looked dead and he wouldn't wake up when we shook him," Mary said.

"And I checked his breath with a mirror and there was no breath," Paddy added.

"Okay," Jack cut in "Let's say he wasn't dead. He gets up and goes to Ron's. Do you know what time that was, Ron?"

"I do," Esther cut in. "It was ten forty-five. I remember because I sprained my ankle and was watching the clock 'til I could take my next pain pill. He made a lot of noise out there."

"Now it's starting to come together." Jack nodded his head. "The timeline makes sense. Tell us what happened when Earl showed up at your place, Ron."

"Well, he smashed into my patio table, causing quite a racket, so I ran outside and there he was, drunk ... at least, I thought he was drunk. Anyway, he started picking a fight with me and I was still mad about the insurance money and all, so we got into it a bit. He was dancing all over the yard, throwing punches and yelling. I hit him and he fell face down in the ditch. It was full of water. I ran down to get him out, but he was too heavy. I thought he was dead, so I ran inside and called Mona."

Nans grimaced. "I must have been too flustered to understand what Ron was saying, what with thinking about hiding the body and all."

"So, then what?" Davies asked. "Did you all drag the body out of the drainage ditch and bring it to McDonalds'?"

Paddy, Ron, and Nans looked at each other.

Nans said, "No, actually it wasn't in the ditch when I saw it—"

"That explains why he was all wet," Floyd cut in.

"What do you mean?"

"When he came crashing around my fence and we got into the fight, I noticed he was wet. I thought it was odd, but you never know with Earl. I just figured he pissed someone off at the bar and they dumped their beer on him," Floyd said.

"And what exactly happened when he came into your yard and why were *you* out there in the middle of the night?" Jack asked.

"Earl and I had an on-going feud because he didn't keep his yard up. As if that wasn't bad enough, he was putting up a fence, but it was well into my yard," Floyd replied. "Anyway, I had seen him out there in the middle of the night a few times and was keeping a watch to try to figure out what he was up to. To this day, I have no idea what he was doing. I'm sure it was something suspicious, though. It looked like he was digging."

"Digging?" Lexy asked remembering how the landlady had said there were holes all over the yard. Earl had been burying something secretly at night and Lexy had a good idea it must have been the money from the insurance scams. But that begged the question ... who dug it up?

"Yes, digging." Floyd answered. "Anyway, that night, I was out on watch and he came along and we got into it. One thing led to another and it came to blows. We were all over the backyards and ended up right in the McDonalds' yard. The funny thing is, I didn't even really punch him. I'd wound up and was in the middle of throwing the punch and then he just fell into it. Passed out drunk ... or so I thought. But then I took his pulse and he didn't have one—he was dead. And that's when Mona and the others came along. I just thought they'd seen what happened and were coming over to help."

"But they weren't. They were coming to hide the body that Paddy thought he killed." Davies looked at Nans, Ron and Paddy. "Didn't you guys wonder what Floyd was doing out there and how the body got there?"

"Actually, I just thought Mona had called everyone and they'd already started to move it," Paddy said.

"Me, too," Ron added.

"I'd called Floyd and let it ring two and a half times. Like I said earlier, that was a signal between us neighbors and it meant to meet in the backyards. Usually, that was just for barbecues or a nightcap. We'd never met to hide a body before. Anyway, when I saw Floyd out there, I just thought Paddy or Ron had clued him in and he'd already started dragging the body down from Sullivan's ... it was only a couple houses down," Nans said.

Wait a minute, didn't you guys talk about the events of the evening and figure out who killed him?" Jack looked at them incredulously.

"Nope," Nans answered for them. "We were too busy. Plus, we wanted to be quiet so we wouldn't wake any of the other neighbors. And afterwards, we vowed never to talk about it again."

"I guess no one felt much like talking about how they'd killed another person, even if it was Earl and mostly in self-defense," Paddy said. "I know I didn't."

"Me, either," Ron agreed.

"Ditto," Floyd added.

"And it was just you four?" Jack asked.

Paddy thrust his chin toward Violet. "And Violet."

Jack's brows drew into a V. "I wondered about her. Where does Violet come in?"

"She showed up when we were moving the body," Paddy said.

"I guess she must have seen us with the body and came over to help." Nans looked over at Violet.

"That's right. I have terrible insomnia and was out walking when I saw the commotion. I knew the folks here and Ron and Esther go to my church, so I just pitched in and helped. You see, I'd had my troubles with Earl, too."

"So, you *did* put the sachets in with him!" Lexy said.

Violet nodded.

"Okay, so then you all dragged him to the McDonalds' basement and started making that secret room?" Davies scrunched up her face. "Why would the McDonalds even agree to that?"

"Well, they were part of our core group. We do everything to help each other out. So, of course they said yes," Esther said.

"Plus they owed me a favor," Nans added.

"Oh?" Davies brows shot up.

"Yes, their oldest got into some trouble and I was able to use my connections to hush it up. It's private and not pertaining to this case, so I'd rather keep the details to myself, if you don't mind," Nans said primly.

"Fair enough ... for now," Jack replied.

"So, anyway," Nans continued. "The McDonalds agreed to call Nesbaum and tell him his services were no longer needed. Then, we all got to work."

"So, just the five of you redid the basement and made that room?" Lexy asked.

"Seven," Nans answered. "Ester and Mary helped, too."

"And you did all the work yourselves?" Jack asked.

"Yep, Paddy and Ron are tradesmen and they knew just how to do it. They supervised and we all got it done in thirty-six hours."

Jacks brows crept up. "And nobody else in the neighborhood noticed what you were doing?"

"Nope, we kept it quite hush-hush. The work was done under the cover of darkness and all."

"What about the smell?" Davies asked. "The body had to have started to smell."

Nans wrinkled her nose. "He did start to smell, especially toward the end. Violet suggested we cover him with lavender sachets. She ran home and got a bunch of them, then she crawled right into that space and laid them all around."

"Took her time and did a nice job, too," Paddy added.

"It didn't work so well, though. The body stunk up the place," Floyd said.

"That's right. Lois tried to cover it up by cooking those spicy foreign dishes." Esther laughed at the memory.

"We ate that stuff for weeks!" Nans said.

"Wait, didn't you say someone's septic system flooded?" Lexy asked.

"Oh, we just made that up when you started asking around in case anyone talked about the smell," Nans said.

"Well, that explains why Ed Johnston didn't know anything about the septic system," Lexy said.

"Oh, right," Nans shrugged. "Ed wasn't part of our little clique. He didn't know anything about what we were doing, so I never talked to him about the plan to cast suspicion away from us."

"So, you guys got together and made up a plan to lie to me, then?" Lexy looked at Nans. "When I started trying to find out about the mummy, I mean."

Nans cheeks turned pink and she looked at her lap. "Yes, dear. I'm sorry, but I felt it was best to protect all of us."

Lexy nodded. That explained a lot about Nans' recent, odd behavior; why she wasn't interested in discussing the case, why she and the Witts had lied about Nans being there and even her secret meeting with Violet.

"By the way, your glasses are at the Witt's," Lexy said. "Even though you said you hadn't been there ... I saw them on the table in the living room. Esther tried to cover for you and claim they were hers."

Nans turned a deeper shade of red and so did Esther.

"Thank you, dear," Nans said meekly.

"I think it's amazing that all these years, no one has said anything." Davies shook her head. "You guys never talked to each other about it? Not even once?"

"Nope," Nans said. "And it turns out no one even missed Earl. We all vowed never to speak of it again, and as far as I know, we've all kept that vow."

Everyone nodded in agreement.

"No wonder the McDonalds wanted to leave everything in the basement when they sold me the house," Jack said. "I thought I was being a nice guy and helping out some elderly folks and I was really helping them keep a body hidden!"

"Oh, they didn't want to sell the house with that body in there," Nans said. "But they had to. Charlie had that problem with his hip and the property taxes were killing them. They were mighty nervous to hear a police detective bought it."

"I'll bet," Jack said.

"That's why I was sent over to make sure you didn't poke around too much," Nans said.

"Oh, and here I thought you just wanted to be friends," Jack said, acting hurt.

Nans flushed. "Well, at first I was just making sure you didn't have plans for the basement. But once I got to know you, I really did want to be friends."

Davies looked down at her notes. "Well, I'm not sure what to make of all this. I was trying to find the murderer to make sure the Feds didn't prosecute the wrong person and I'm not sure I like what I found."

"Oh, that's right." Nans turned sorrowful eyes on Floyd. "It sounds like Floyd actually killed him. He won't have to go to jail, will he?"

"I dont know..." Davies looked at Jack.

"I think—" Violet started.

"Well, I'm not so sure it was Floyd," Jack cut in. "The way Floyd mentions him just falling, it could have been one of the blows he received earlier which caused some kind of blood clot or brain swelling and he just happened to die in front of Floyd. He was walking around like he was drunk, but he might have had a concussion from when Paddy hit him."

"Or maybe even from his fight with Ron," Lexy suggested.

"So, which one of us really killed him, then?" Floyd asked.

"Maybe they can figure that out through the autopsy," Nans suggested. "But I hate to think of any one one of us going to jail. If one goes, we all go. Isn't that right?"

Everyone murmured their agreement.

Violet spoke up, "I must tell you—"

She was interrupted by the door whipping open. A tall man with a gleaming FBI badge nestled on the hip of his black dress pants stepped in.

"No one is going to go to jail," he said. "At least not for killing Earl Schute. Because you're not the ones that actually killed him."

Chapter Twenty-Four

Everyone stared at the man. He was tall and broad-shouldered, his face worn with lines, his dark hair graying at the temples. Lexy could tell he'd been on the job for a while and he meant business.

"What? Of course we killed him." Floyd broke the silence, sounding almost indignant.

"Yeah, we buried him. He was dead. I saw it with my own eyes," Ron added.

"Oh, he was dead all right. It's just that he didn't die from a punch or a blow from a baseball bat," the man said.

Nans fixed him with a steely glare. "And just *who* are you, anyway?"

"*And* how did you find out about this meeting?" Davies added angrily.

The man shrugged. "I have my ways."

Davies sighed. "This is detective Binder of the FBI."

Davies made a round of introductions and Binder pulled a chair up to the table.

"So, you knew we were meeting the whole time?" Davies asked. "How?"

"We're the Feds, we know everything," Binder said importantly. "Our sources told us you were having this soiree and we bugged the room. We figured no one would open up to *us* and we'd have a better chance of finding out the truth if we listened in. Anyway, we just got the full autopsy report back and Earl wasn't killed by fighting with any of you."

Davies brows rose. "Well, what killed him, then?"

"Poison."

"What?" Paddy Sullivan's forehead collapsed in layers of wrinkles. "How could that be? He was walking around fine. If he ate something poisonous, wouldn't he have died where he ate it or at least have been physically sick?"

"It wasn't *ingested*, it was *injected*," Binder replied.

"What? How?" Davies asked.

"And when?" Jack added.

Binder shrugged. "*That*, we're not sure about. The autopsy revealed traces of aconite in his tissue. It's a poison. We think it may have been injected through a tiny pinhole in his neck, but it's hard to tell, given the condition of his skin."

"If someone injected him with a needle, why would he be just walking around the neighborhood?" Floyd asked.

"Maybe the poison made him delirious or something before he died," Ron suggested. "He *was* acting strange."

"Nope, that's the thing. That kind of poison would kill him pretty much instantly."

"Instantly?" Nans chewed her bottom lip. "But Floyd was the last one to see him alive."

Everyone looked at Floyd, who spread his hands. "I didn't inject him with any poison. Did you see any syringes on me? I wouldn't even know how to use one."

"You wouldn't need to use a hypodermic. Just a prick of a needle with concentrated aconite on it could do the trick." Binder glared at him. "Do you have a garden?"

"What?" Floyd looked at him like he was crazy. "No!"

"Why do you ask that?" Nans asked.

"The aconite comes from a plant. The wolfsbane plant," Binder replied. "But we don't think it was Floyd or any of you, anyway."

"Oh, well, that's a relief," Nans said.

"So, you think it was one of the other people he scammed, then?" Davies asked.

"Scammed?" Binder's brows creased for a second. "Oh, you mean that insurance thing. No, that's not why we're interested in, Earl."

"Why are you, then?" Jack asked.

"Earl Schute was in the witness protection program. We lost track of him in nineteen-fifty-five. When we heard his body had surfaced, we had to come check it out." Binder squirmed in his seat and glanced at the door. "You see, our department was the one that lost track of Earl and it's been a black mark on us ever since. We get the crappiest cases—the bottom of the barrel—because of it. Of course, I wasn't around then, but if I could close the case, it might redeem our status."

"Witness protection?" Nans stared at Binder. "Why was he in there? Was he some kind of gangster?"

Binder nodded. "He ratted out his boss and we put him in protection."

"I knew there was something odd about him," Esther Witt said. "That explains the way he acted."

"But what do you need to solve?" Nans asked. "I mean, now you know where he is and that he's been dead all this time."

"Earl testified against the mob boss, Harry Gooch. We think Harry sent one of his guys to kill him," Binder said. "A particular assassin who used this type of poison. That assassin has been on our Most Wanted list for sixty years and if we could find him, that would go a long way toward raising the status of my department."

"You think the assassin is still around?" Violet asked. "It's been decades. He's probably dead by now."

"Maybe. But the mystery is that this particular assassin who has this M.O. disappeared the same time Earl did. I need to find out what happened to him, whether he is dead or alive."

"M.O.?" Nans perked up. "What exactly was his M.O.?"

"He usually stalks his victim and kills using this poison. But the thing is, he doesn't need to get near the victim—he shoots a poison dart. Then he cuts off a body part and sends it back for proof."

"The toe!" Lexy blurted out.

Binder nodded. "Yep, Earl's toe was cut off post-mortem. We think it was by this assassin."

"And you think the assassin is one of us?" Floyd asked.

"No, that's the thing. We checked you all out and you' all lived here long before Earl showed up. Plus, we don't show any of you traveling to the areas the assassin made his kills in. The assassin would have had a big deposit in his bank account after Earl's kill was verified and none of you have that."

"Well, that's a relief," Floyd said. "And here all these years I thought I'd killed a man."

"Me, too," Ron echoed.

Paddy nodded. "As did I."

"The thing is, very little is known about this guy," Binder continued. "We call him Blow Gun Bennie because of the methods he uses. We don't know his real name and no one has ever seen him. He's been very clever."

"Well, I'm just glad it wasn't one of us," Nans said. "And we don't have to go to jail."

"Oh, I didn't say you weren't going to jail. I just said you weren't going for *murder*." Binder leaned back in his chair. "But you're all accessories. After all, you did dispose of the body and that *is* against the law."

"Oh, dear." Nans looked at him with wide eyes. "So you're going to incarcerate all of us?"

"Well, I *could* ... but I might be able to convince the judge to go easy on you if you help me out."

"How can we help you?" Nans asked.

"You were all out there that night when Earl died. The assassin was out there, too. If any of you can give me information that helps us uncover the identity of the assassin, then I'll make sure you all get off with probation and community service."

"Well, obviously the assassin must have been the stranger," Lexy blurted out.

"Stranger?" Nans looked at her quizzically, then her brows shot up. "Oh, yes, how could I forget? You all remember the stranger that was around the neighborhood back then, right?"

The others nodded.

Binder's brows shot up and he leaned in toward the middle of the table. "Tell me about him. What did he look like?"

They all talked at once.

"Tall."

"Medium."

"Blonde."

"Dark."

Binder's brows crept higher on his forehead with each person's description. "That sounds like more than one person. But our sources tell us he may have been a master of disguise. Maybe he just changed his look so no one could describe him."

Nans nodded. "That's probably it."

"Did any of you talk to him?" Binder asked.

They glanced at each other and Nans spoke. "I don't believe so. We all just kind of saw him lurking around."

"Where?"

"On the street and in the yards."

"Did it seem like he was stalking Earl?"

"Now that you mention it, I think he was." Nans turned to Paddy, Ron and Floyd. "Don't you guys think he was?"

"Oh, yeah," Paddy said.

"Yep," came from Ron.

"I'm pretty sure I saw him poking around Earl's yard," Floyd added.

"How long was he around?"

"Just a few weeks that summer." Nans scrunched up her face in thought. "It wasn't more than two weeks."

Binder pressed his lips together, and his eyes sparked. "This could be our guy."

"Yes," Nans said. "I do believe you could be right because I don't recall seeing him at all after Earl died."

"Is that right?" Binder looked at Paddy, Ron, Floyd and Violet.

"Yep, I didn't see him after," Paddy said.

Ron looked at Esther. "I don't remember seeing him after Earl died, do you?"

She shook her head. "Nope."

"Me, either, Violet said.

"Nor me," Floyd added.

"So, you see, we've solved the mystery." Nans looked at Binder. "So you'll help us avoid jail time, like you said?"

"No. I said I'd help you if you gave us information that helped us uncover the *identity* of the assassin. You've only verified a stranger was on the street. That doesn't help us figure out who he is."

Nans bristled. "Well, how are we supposed to help you do that?"

Binder stood up. "Give us something concrete to go on and then I'll think about helping you."

He walked toward the door and had it halfway open when Nans asked; "What do you mean by concrete?"

Binder turned. "Something tangible. A clue that leads me to a person. But you'd better hurry. You only have two days and after that, the deal is off."

And with that, Binder stepped out into the hall and closed the door, leaving them all looking at each other and wondering how in the world they were going to come up with a concrete clue in only two days.

Chapter Twenty-Five

Lexy, Nans and the neighbors headed to *The Cup and Cake,* which they hoped the FBI hadn't bugged. They didn't want them to overhear their conversation. Davies and Jack had police business to attend to, so it was only Lexy, Nans, Violet, the Sullivan's, the Witt's and Floyd Nichols. They pulled two tables together and sat down to discuss their plan.

Lexy tingled with anxiety—she should have been in the kitchen, focusing on her meringue cookie recipes for the dessert contest, but instead she was out here, seated across from her rival, Violet Switzer, and trying to keep Nans out of jail.

She glanced at Violet out of the corner of her eye. Was she scoping out the bakery? Lexy hoped the older woman wouldn't find something in here to use against her and get a leg up in the contest, but the truth was that Violet's demeanor had changed since the meeting at the police station. She wasn't combative or snarky anymore—quite the contrary. Lexy hated to say it, but Violet was acting nice. Then again, maybe that was part of her plan to throw Lexy off-kilter.

"What does he mean by something concrete?" Paddy asked as he bit into an almond scone.

"I guess something physical, that you can hold in your hand," Floyd answered.

"Or maybe a lead to a real person, like an address or something," Esther suggested.

"Well, it's going to be kind of hard to get anything like that," Ron said.

Lexy nodded. "Right, because it happened over fifty years ago and any physical evidence of the stranger would be gone by now."

"Well, that ..." Nans looked at Lexy and grimaced. "And also because there was no stranger."

Lexy jerked her head back. Had she heard Nans correctly? "What?"

"We made it up," Nans confessed.

Lexy's brows drew together. "Why?"

"When I heard Earl's body had been discovered, I knew someone would come asking questions. So I high-tailed it over to the McDonalds', then to Floyd, Paddy and Ron and we agreed to pretend we all saw a stranger. That way, we could act like the stranger had killed Earl."

"Except we forgot to get together on the description," Mary said.

"We never dreamed there really *was* another person ... we thought one of us killed him!" Nans added.

"But if there was no actual stranger, then who really killed Earl?" Lexy looked around the table, but everyone seemed just as perplexed as she was as to who the real killer could be.

Nans shrugged. "Your guess is as good as mine. I guess the assassin really was lurking around and we didn't know it at the time."

"Right," Ron said. "Binder said this Blow Gun Bennie shoots the darts from a distance. He must have been hiding behind the houses and shot Earl when he was fighting with Floyd."

"That would explain why you thought Earl had fallen into the punch," Nans said to Floyd. "He really did fall and he was already dead before his face hit your hand."

Floyd shuddered. "Well, I'm glad Bennie had good aim. He could have missed and hit me."

"Yeah, but the problem still remains," Paddy said. "How are we going to get this concrete evidence Binder wants?"

Violet, who had been quietly listening, said matter-of-factly, "We'll just have to manufacture it."

Floyd looked at her over the rim of his coffee cup. "Now, Violet, I don't know if you want to get involved. If the Feds catch us manufacturing evidence to support our lie about this stranger, we could be in even more trouble than we already are. And you weren't even involved in killing Earl ... why, you just happened across us that night and helped us out in an act of neighborly kindness."

"We're in this together now. I'm not going to abandon you." Violet's voice shook and Lexy thought she saw tears in the old curmudgeon's eyes. "Why, the way you all stuck up for each other in that meeting and refused to let one person be singled out to go to jail makes me proud to be associated with you. I wish I hadn't moved away all those years ago and had gotten to know you all better."

"Well, you can still get to know us, dear," Mary said. "You're invited to our place any time you want to visit."

"Which will be in the state penitentiary if we don't get Binder this evidence he wants," Ron said dryly.

"And that brings us back to the question." Floyd put his coffee mug on the table and sat back in his chair. "Just how are we going to do that?"

Nans pressed her lips together. "We need something from back then. Something we can tie to the murder that will point to another person."

"A scapegoat?" Violet asked.

"Yes," Nans answered. "But not some innocent, unsuspecting person—a criminal—someone who deserves to get blamed for being an assassin."

"And someone who is dead with no chance of proving their innocence," Violet added.

"That sounds great," Paddy said. "But where are we going to find physical evidence linking to Earl's murder?"

"Don't worry," Nans said, "I think I have an idea."

Chapter Twenty-Six

The next day, Lexy stood in the front room of *The Cup and Cake,* eyeing the plate of meringue cookies nervously. She was supposed to be working on perfecting her recipe for the dessert contest, but instead, she was waiting for Nans to pick her up for the trip to the police station.

With a sigh, she poured some hot water into a mug and dunked a chamomile tea pouch into the steaming water. It had been a harrowing morning. Ruth, Ida and Helen had marched in with their noses still out of joint about missing the meeting at the police station the day before. They couldn't understand why Davies hadn't invited them.

It had taken Lexy two hours and over a dozen pastries to soothe their ruffled feathers and they'd finally calmed down while Lexy filled them in on the exact details of the meeting.

They'd been shocked to find out the real truth, and even more shocked to hear Lexy say she thought Violet wasn't all that bad.

"Not that bad?" Ida's blue eyes looked like a storm at sea. "You just wait and see. I wouldn't trust her. You'll find out tomorrow at the dessert contest."

The three women had bustled out to go to hair appointments, leaving Lexy on her own. She tapped her finger impatiently against her teacup and worried what Violet might do at the dessert contest as she waited for Nans.

A blur of red whipped around the corner and Lexy's eyes grew wide as Violet Switzer's Mustang squealed to a stop in front of the bakery. The passenger door opened and Nans gingerly stepped out and opened the bakery door, her gaze scanning the room and then stopping at the stunned Lexy, still rooted in her chair.

"Oh, hi, Lexy." Nans gestured toward the door. "Are you ready?"

"We're going with Violet?"

"Yes, dear. Violet helped me out. I think we have just what Binder wants." Nans winked and held the door open, gesturing for Lexy to get a move on.

"What is it?" Lexy put her teacup in the dirty cup bin and walked toward the door.

"Oh, now, I don't want to spoil the surprise."

Lexy narrowed her eyes at Nans and then called to Cassie over her shoulder. "Cassie, I'm taking off."

"Okay. Good luck, Mona!" Cassie's voice rang out from the back room.

"Thanks!" Nans yelled back as she ushered Lexy outside and into the back seat of the Mustang.

Lexy settled into the soft leather and looked up to see Violet angling the rear-view mirror to look at her. Lexy stared into her piercing, blue eyes. Not twinkling blue like Nans were, though. Violet's eyes were still and dark, like a shark.

Violet smiled, but the corners of her eyes did't crinkle. "I just wanted to tell you, I think if you use a little bit more cream of tartar in your meringue cookies, you might have a good chance of winning the contest."

Then she snapped the mirror back up, cut her eyes to the road, gunned the Mustang out of its parking spot and sped off toward the police station.

Violet had a lead foot and Lexy felt nauseous by the time they arrived. She wasn't sure if it was Violet's speed-racer driving, the fact that she'd gotten advice from her on baking, or the anticipation of what might happen if Binder didn't buy into Nans' evidence.

Paddy, Mary, Ron, Esther and Floyd were waiting for them in the lobby and Davies brought them to the same room they'd been in the day before. Binder was sitting at the head of the table, eyeing them curiously as they marched in and took their seats.

"So, did you find something for me?" Binder asked.

Nans produced a brown paper shopping bag and handed it to him. "I believe what you need is in here."

Binder peered inside. His brows knit together. He reached in and pulled something out. Lexy's stomach tightened when she recognized the red flip-flop that had been in her garage. Binder set it on the table, then pulled out another item—a black wig.

"I don't get it. How will these help me?" he asked.

Nans looked at the others for encouragement and they nodded at her.

"I told a little lie yesterday," Nans started.

Binder's left brow ticked up. "Just one?"

Nans grimaced. "Well, you see, it was very confusing the night Earl died. Everything happened so fast. And it did happen the way we told you except I left one thing out."

"Go on," Binder prompted.

"After we dragged Earl into the basement and did some cover up, we all went back to our houses. The sun was coming up and we didn't want neighbors who were leaving for work early to see us."

Binder made circling motions with his finger. "... And?" He drew the word out into several syllables.

"Well, I was walking through the McDonalds' backyard to my house when I heard something behind me. We didn't have the fence up in those days, so our backyards were one big grassy area. Anyway, I turned to see what the noise was and it was the stranger. He had that red flip-flop and I recognized it as Earl's. I didn't know who he was or what he wanted with it, but I knew I didn't want him to have it. I was afraid he was some kind of blackmailer and would use it against us. So I launched myself at him and wrestled him for it." Nans face flushed. "I'm embarrassed to admit I was a bit of a dirty fighter back in the day, and I kicked and scratched and I might even have punched him in a place where men don't like to be punched. Anyway, he let go of the shoe, and in the struggle, his wig came off. Then he ran away and I never saw him again."

"So you fought with this stranger and then you never told your accomplices?" Binder said pointing to the others.

"No. I didn't want them to get upset if they knew someone had witnessed what we had done."

"And you kept the shoe and wig all this time?"

Nans nodded. "I hid them in my garage ... well, it's Lexy's garage now. I sold my house to her."

Lexy's stomach dropped. She hadn't seen any wig in the garage with the red flip-flop. Had it been there the whole time or had Nans gotten it from someone else?"

Binder poked at the flip-flop with his pencil. "Well, this definitely looks like Earl's missing flip-flop."

"Maybe Blow Gun Bennie had it after he cut off Earl's toe," Paddy suggested.

"Maybe," Binder said.

"He was wearing the wig," Nans pointed at the wig. "It could have DNA evidence that might help you identify who he was."

"Right, if this person actually was Blow Gun Bennie." Binder sounded skeptical.

"I can't imagine who else it could have been," Nans said. "I mean, who else would be out there with Earl's flip flop other than the assassin?"

Binder nodded. "You have a point. I'll get these to the lab for DNA testing."

"And if it helps you find the assassin's identity, will we get off on probation?" Mary asked hopefully.

Binder narrowed his eyes. "I'll do what I can. I'll put a rush on this. In the meantime, you people can go. But don't go far ... you're not in the clear by any stretch of the imagination and we still have the little matter of moving a body and tampering with evidence to settle."

***

After Binder dismissed them, the group went their separate ways. Violet dropped Lexy off at the bakery, where she tried to remain focused on perfecting the meringues recipe for the contest the next day.

Three hours into it, she was staring at her last bowl of meringue batter. She'd fiddled with the amount of vanilla extract and added just a quarter teaspoon more sugar. The addition of the sugar made her nervous, but pretty much everyone had said they needed more. Besides, could there ever be such a thing as a dessert that was too sweet?

She grabbed the piping bag, then her eye fell on the cream of tartar. Violet's advice echoed in her head. She reluctantly added a pinch, then beat the batter until it was shiny. Finally, she folded in some miniature chocolate chips and chopped pecans, then filled the piping bag and pushed the batter out into perfectly peaked cookies, which she slid gently into the oven.

Setting the timer, she went out front to check the bakery cases and was just moving some fig squares to the top shelf when the door burst open and Nans came through, waving a paper in her hand.

"It's over!" Nans yelled, her face flushed with excitement. "We helped the Feds solve the case!"

"You did?" Lexy's brows dipped together. "You mean the evidence you gave Binder really panned out?"

"Yep. And he talked to Judge Hastings, who is going to give us all community service and no jail time. I need a double chocolate frosted brownie to celebrate."

Relief flooded through Lexy as she picked the largest brownie from the case and handed it to Nans.

"Thanks!" Nans grabbed the brownie and turned to leave.

"Wait a minute." Lexy was relieved that Nans and her neighbors weren't going to jail, but even if the Feds were satisfied with the evidence they got, Lexy still had a lot of unanswered questions, not the least of which was how Nans' trumped up evidence ended in them finding the real assassin. "I don't understand. How did you manage to get that wig from the assassin? Did you really see him that night?"

Nans stopped and took a step back toward Lexy. She leaned across the bakery case and whispered In Lexy's ear. "I never said the wig was from the actual assassin. Does it really matter? The DNA was from a deceased party who *could* be the assassin and the murder was decades ago. As long as an innocent person doesn't go to jail for it, I think that's all that matters at this point, don't you?"

"I guess so," Lexy said, "But where did you get a wig from a deceased assassin?"

But Nans had already turned and had made it to the door with record speed. "Sorry, I can't stay ... I gotta give the others the good news!"

And with that, she was out the door and hopping into Violet's red Mustang.

With a shrug, Lexy turned back to the bakery case. Nans was right. After all this time, it didn't really matter if they caught the assassin. What mattered was that Nans and her neighbors weren't going to jail and the case was closed.

Now, Lexy could focus on winning the dessert contest. After all, she had more important things to do than find out the identity of the real assassin, didn't she?

Chapter Twenty-Seven

"So, this Binder fellow let you all off with just community service?" Ida's eyes were wide as she studied Nans who'd just filled Ida, Ruth and Helen in on how she'd handed over the flip-flop and wig to Binder.

"Yep, he said the DNA on the wig led him to a well-known criminal." Nans looked up at the ceiling. "Marco somebody or other."

"But *where* did you get the flip-flop and the wig?" Ruth whispered, glancing around to make sure no one in the Grange Hall was seated near enough to hear.

Which they weren't because the Grange Hall was abuzz with the activity of the Brook Ridge Falls Dessert contest and no one was paying attention to the four old ladies and Lexy who were at a table in the back. People were more interested in the judges, who sat at a long table in the front of the hall, plates filled with dessert samples in front of them. Contestants swarmed in with their entries that were placed on a table for everyone to see. The smell of sugar, cinnamon and chocolate spiced the air.

Lexy had already dropped her cookies at the table and was now dividing her attention between the judges, who were tasting the entries, and Nans and the ladies.

"I thought you made up the whole thing about the stranger," Helen was saying.

"I did," Nans replied in hushed tones. "I really *didn't* see any stranger that night, but I did find the flip-flop. It was in the backyard between my house and the McDonalds'. It must have fallen off. I didn't really know what to do with it, but I figured I couldn't leave it lying outside so I hid it in the garage. Good thing, too, because it sure came in handy."

Ruth scrunched up her face. "But there must have been a stranger because *someone* had to have shot that dart at Earl."

Nans nodded. "You're right. Someone else must have been there, but we just didn't see him. I mean, if you were a hired assassin, you'd probably be pretty good at concealing yourself, right?"

"True." Ruth scrunched her face in thought. "There's one thing I was wondering, though. How did this Marco guy get that concentrated poison?"

"You mean aconite?" Helen asked. "Why, that's easy. You can grow it right in your garden. It comes from the Wolfsbane plant. When harvested in a certain way, it can be very poisonous."

"Oh." Ida made a face. "Now that you mention it, I think I saw that on TV. What I don't understand is who dug up Earl's yard and what was buried there?"

"You mean the round holes?" Helen asked. "I was thinking about that and it reminded me of my crazy Uncle Louie who used to bury money in mason jars around his yard. He didn't trust banks."

"Maybe Earl buried the money from the insurance scams in his yard," Ruth suggested. "We didn't find any bank accounts where he deposited that money and he probably wouldn't have trusted the bank, either."

"Especially since he was in the witness protection program," Helen agreed. "They probably monitor that stuff."

"Maybe this assassin knew and dug the money up," Ida suggested.

Ruth nodded. "It makes sense the assassin would have known. He was probably watching Earl—stalking him, you know, so he could plan a good time for the kill. The money was untraceable cash. It would have been an added bonus for killing Earl that no one would even know he had."

"Boy, this assassin must have walked away with a windfall," Ida exclaimed. "What with the money for killing Earl and the insurance money he dug up in the yard."

"I'll say." Ruth turned to Nans. "And you say it was this Marco guy? Did the Feds check his bank accounts and find he had that insurance money? Some of that was yours, Mona, so maybe you could get it back."

Nans waved her hand in the air. "Oh, I wouldn't even try. I'm happy just leaving the past behind me now."

Ida narrowed her eyes. "But I still don't understand. Where did you get the wig?"

Nans glanced around uneasily. "Oh, well, I really can't say about that."

Lexy eyed her grandmother curiously. "But how did you guys get the wig to have DNA samples from this mobster?"

Nans gave Lexy her most innocent look. "I really don't know. My source has connections and they wouldn't tell me much more."

"And he really was the killer?" Ida asked.

Nans shrugged. "I'm not sure. He's been dead for years and he *was* a hired killer, but as to whether or not he was *Earl's* killer, I don't know. But what does it matter? That's old history now."

"What I don't understand is why the Feds didn't think one of you guys was the assassin," Helen said.

"They checked us all out, and since we'd all lived in town long before Earl came along, and none of us had traveled on the dates of other killings, they knew it wasn't us," Nans replied.

"Well, they must not have checked very hard," Ida said.

Nans looked puzzled. "Why do you say that?"

"There's one person in your group who didn't live in town before Earl came along," Ida replied.

"Really? Who?" Nans asked.

Ida cut her eyes over to the front of the room where Violet Switzer sat, chatting with two other ladies.

Nans followed her gaze. "You mean Violet? She used to live downtown before she moved to our neighborhood. What makes you say she hasn't lived here?"

"I decided to check her out while I was looking into the case," Ida said. "Violet and I have a history and I was curious. Anyway, it seems she hasn't lived in Brook Ridge Falls as long as she says she has."

"I'm not sure what you mean." Nans narrowed her eyes at Ida. "How is that possible?"

"Seems she faked some records," Ruth cut in. "If you do a preliminary search, it appears as if she lived in town for decades before Earl was killed, but if you know where to dig, you'll find she showed up just the same time Earl did."

"Huh ... We'll, I'll be." Nans paused for a moment, then shrugged. "Well anyway, the Feds seemed pretty sure the assassin was this Marco guy and all the rest of us have to do is satisfy our community service requirements and stay out of trouble."

"You're lucky you aren't going to jail for it."

"I know, but I do have a record now," Nans said, sounding almost proud of it.

"Uh-oh, are you violating your probation or something?" Ruth asked.

"What? No, why?"

Ruth thrust her chin in the direction of the door and they all turned to see Watson Davies striding toward them.

"Well, I'm happy to report Binder and his people have packed up and left." Davies sat down next to Nans. "I'm glad to have him out of my hair."

"Me, too," Nans said wryly.

"You got off easy, Mona." Davies gave Nans a stern look and Nans' cheeks turned pink.

"What kind of service do you have to do?" Helen asked.

"I have to stock shelves in the town library for a month," Nans replied.

"That doesn't sound too bad," Ida said. "What did your cohorts get?"

"Paddy and Mary have thirty days trash pickup on route five, Ron has to renovate the mayor's office, Esther has to knit scarves for the councilmen, Violet is teaching a gardening class at the women's prison, and Floyd is teaching fishing classes at the Y."

"But, I wonder, Mona, how did you come up with that evidence?" Davies turned sharp eyes on Nans. "If you'd had that wig all along, I'm sure you would have produced it. You might fool Binder, but you can't fool me."

"Oh, well, you're right about the wig—I didn't have it. I'm sorry, though, dear. I can't tell you my secrets. After all, the judge said the case is closed now and I think it's best we don't talk about it anymore, especially not in public."

Davies turned to Lexy. "At least Jack's house is cleared and you can finish cleaning it out and get it on the market."

Lexy's stomach pinched. "Yeah, if anyone wants to buy a house that had a mummy in it. I don't have high hopes on that one and I was counting on the money from the sale to pay my parents back on my bakery loan."

"Well, you might be in luck." Davies pulled a business card out of her pocket and slid it across the table to Lexy. "This is a friend of mine. He's a ghost hunter and he's very interested in Jack's house because of the mummy."

"Really?" Lexy raised her brows. "That would be great. I think my parents need the money to fix their RV."

"No, they don't," Nans cut in. "I got a text from Vera this morning. They got that old part you sent and the RV is running good as new. In fact, they're leaving Maine and are on their way to Alamo Heights, Texas, to visit the toilet seat museum."

Davies made a face. "Toilet seat museum?"

Nans shrugged, "What can I say. They like to visit strange places." Nans turned to Lexy. "I didn't realize you were in that old storage area in the garage. You didn't find anything strange in there when you got that part out did you?"

Lexy narrowed her eyes, wondering why Nans was asking. Everyone already knew the flip-flop had been hidden in there ... unless there was something else in there Nans didn't want her to see. "What do you mean?"

"Oh, nothing ... just that ... we'll that's where the flip-flop was."

Lexy had the distinct impression Nans was hiding something, but she didn't have the chance to think about it, because she could see the judges out of the corner of her eye and they were tasting the last dish—her meringue cookies.

Lexy focused her attention on the front of the room, trying to gauge the judge's' reactions to her cookies, but their faces didn't give anything away— Lexy wondered if they all played poker in their spare time.

Finally, they pushed away their plates and Miriam Hash, the town clerk and head judge, stood up at the podium. She tapped the microphone, causing an ear-shattering screech to fill the room.

All talking ceased while heads jerked in Miriam's direction.

"Thank you, everyone," Mariam trilled into the microphone. "Welcome to the tenth Brook Ridge Falls Dessert contest."

Lexy tapped her foot impatiently while Miriam introduced the judges and went through her spiel about the contest and the various entries. Finally, Joan Barnstead stood up with the ribbons and handed Miriam a piece of paper. Miriam settled blue, half-moon glasses on her nose, looked at the paper and took the yellow third-place ribbon from Joan.

Lexy held her breath.

"And now, I would like to announce our winners." Miriam paused for effect and Lexy thought her lungs would burst. "In third place is Agnes Flint with her rhubarb meringue pie."

The room erupted in applause and a small, gray-haired lady shuffled up to get her ribbon and shake hands with the judges.

Miriam waited for Agnes to sit down and then she took the red ribbon from Joan. "In second place ... Lexy Baker, with her meringue cookies!"

Lexy's breath whooshed out and she tried to hide the disappointment on her face.

Second place!

She knew she should have been grateful, but she was a baker, for crying out loud. She should have won. Lexy glared at Violet, who was watching her intently, and wondered if the older woman had paid off the judges. She'd seen her bribe the town hall clerk, so it wouldn't have surprised her.

But, it was too late now and she'd just look like a sore loser if she tried to cast any accusations Violet's way. Besides, she didn't even know if Violet would win.

Lexy pasted a smile on her face, collected the ribbon and the judges' congratulations and sat back down, the ribbon clenched tightly in her fist.

"Congratulations!" Ida, Ruth, Helen, Davies and Nans chorused.

"Thanks," Lexy said, managing a tight smile.

Miriam cleared her throat and Lexy glanced down at her disappointing red ribbon.

Oh, well, second place was still pretty good, wasn't it?

Lexy straightened in her seat, vowing to be grateful for what she had instead of moaning about not getting first place.

Miriam squinted at the paper. Joanne slapped the blue ribbon into Miriam's outstretched hand.

Miriam held it up in front of her. "And the first place prize goes to ..."

The room fell silent.

"Violet Switzer and her lemon meringue pie!"

Violet stormed up to the podium amidst the applause. Lexy was surprised to see her grab Miriam in a bear hug ... or so it appeared. But from where Lexy was sitting, she could see that Violet was whispering in Miriam's ear and slipping a note into her hand. Miriam's forehead wrinkled and she looked at what was in her hand, then her face turned white.

Miriam straightened the jacket of her navy polyester suit and grabbed the microphone. "Ahem ... I've just been advised that there is a slight change in the contest winners ... err ... there's actually a tie for first place so the ribbon goes to both Violet Switzer and Lexy Baker!"

Violet ripped the ribbon out of Miriam's hand and broke out into the first genuine smile Lexy had seen since she'd known her. Then she stormed toward Lexy holding the ribbon high.

Violet thrust the ribbon out at Lexy. "You deserve to share this ribbon with me."

Lexy stared at Violet, perplexed. "Why?"

"After what we've been through," Violet nodded toward Nans, "I feel like we're on the same team. Besides, your cookies probably would have won except they had a tad too much sugar. I'm proud to be splitting the ribbon with you."

Lexy was too taken aback at the shimmer of tears in Violet's eyes to say anything. She watched as Violet whipped out a pair of pinking shears and clicked them open. Lexy noticed they were very large —industrial-sized with fancy, curved blades that glimmered in the light while Violet worked the shears to cut the ribbon in half.

Something niggled at Lexy's memory.

Then she remembered how Davies had said Earl's toe had been cut off, with curly-blade pinking shears. Her stomach dropped as she watched the blade of the shears slice through the ribbon, cutting into the thick steel ring at the top like it was butter.

Her thoughts drifted to Violet's garden and she remembered the purple flowers. She was pretty sure one of them was Wolfsbane.

Lexy's mouth dropped open as she stared up at Violet.

Violet had access to a poisonous plant.

Violet had industrial strength, curly pinking shears.

Violet had moved to the neighborhood the same time as Earl and tried to cover her tracks.

Violet was the last person to see Earl's body in the secret room when she jumped in to place the lavender sachets.

Violet had appeared out of nowhere right after Earl dropped dead.

Violet had moved into an expensive new house after Earl died.

Violet was an excellent pea-shooter and could easily have shot a dart at Earl ...

Lexy jerked her head to look at Nans, remembering Nans' words from the day before about the wig not being from the actual assassin.

Lexy shot her hand out and grabbed Nans arm. "I think I know who the real assassin is—"

"Shush, now." Lexy's eyes met Nans. Her grandmother was giving her 'the look'. The one that meant she was deadly serious and Lexy should shut up and pay attention. That look had worked like gangbusters when she was a kid, and it worked now, too. Lexy shut her mouth.

"It won't do to go around casting accusations now," Nans said. "The case is closed. And some things from the past are better left in the past."

Violet handed Lexy her half of the ribbon, winked and stomped off. Lexy stared after her.

Could Violet have been the real assassin and, if she was, should Lexy say something?

Lexy looked back at Nans, who shook her head sagely and put her index finger to her lips.

Lexy's teeth worried her bottom lip as she weighed the situation. Nans was right. There was no sense in dragging that all up now, and if Nans thought she should keep her mouth shut, then that's what Lexy would do. She'd always followed her grandmother's advice before and it had never steered her wrong.

Her thoughts were interrupted by Ruth, who said, "Oh, Mona, here comes your new boyfriend."

"Boyfriend?" Nans swiveled in the direction of Ruth's gaze where a tall, dapper, white-haired man in a bolo tie was scanning the room.

"Oh, that's not my new boyfriend. That's our new client." Nans said waving her hand in the air to attract his attention.

Ida's forehead creased. "But that's the square-dancing guy you've been sneaking off to meet."

"Yeah, I met him at the square dance. And we have been meeting," Nans laughed. "You guys thought I was having a fling with him?"

Ida, Ruth and Helen nodded.

"Sorry to disappoint you. I've been meeting him about a *case*. His sister was killed and he fears the police botched the investigation." Nans face turned serious. "And he greatly needs our help because he thinks he might be the killer's next victim."

"Oh, really?" Ruth's brows rose with interest, and she whipped out her iPad and set it on the table. "I'm ready to take down the preliminaries."

"Well, I'm glad to see you're ready to tackle a case again, Mona," Ida said. "You had us worried there for a while."

"A new case would be very exciting." Helen self-consciously patted the sides of her hair as she eyed the man approaching the table. "Introduce us to your friend."

The introductions were made and Ida started peppering the man for information on the case while Ruth typed it all down on the iPad.

Lexy felt a sense of closure as she stared down at her half of the blue ribbon. Everything was going to work out okay. Nans was back to her old self and interested in cases, she had a lead on a buyer for Jacks house, her parents' RV was running well again, and she had almost won first prize in the dessert contest.

And as for Violet Switzer being Earl's real assassin ... well, maybe Nans was right and some things from the past really were better left in the past.

The end.

***

Want to read about more of Lexy's and Nans' adventures? Get the rest of the Lexy Baker series for your Kindle:

Save 30% when you buy the Lexy Baker Cozy Mystery Boxed Set:

Lexy Baker Cozy Mystery Series Boxed Set Vol 1 (Books 1-4)

Or buy the books separately:

Killer Cupcakes
Dying For Danish

Murder, Money and Marzipan
3 Bodies and a Biscotti
Brownies, Bodies & Bad Guys
Bake, Battle & Roll
Wedded Blintz
Scones, Skulls & Scams
Ice Cream Murder

Sign up for my newsletter and get my books at the lowest discount price:

http://www.leighanndobbs.com/newsletter

Chocolate Chocolate Chip Meringue Cookie Recipe

These cookies have a double dose of chocolate from the batter and the chips. You could vary them by using white chocolate chips, or not adding the cocoa powder to the batter ... or both! Why not try them with butterscotch chips? You can also add chopped nuts.

Ingredients:

3 egg whites
1/8 teaspoon cream of tartar
1/2 teaspoon vanilla extract
2/3 cup sugar
1/2 cup chocolate chips
2 tablespoons unsweetened cocoa powder

Procedure:

Make sure egg whites are at room temperature.

Preheat oven to 250 degrees(F).

Combine egg whites, cream of tartar and vanilla. Beat until soft peaks are formed (about 4 or 5 minutes).

While still beating, slowly add sugar, then beat until mixture becomes glossy and stiff peaks are formed.

Fold in cocoa and chocolate chips.

Push batter onto parchment-lined cookie sheet and put in oven on middle rack. Reduce heat to 200 degrees(F) at once. Bake for 25 to 30 minutes. Turn off oven and let it cool before removing cookies.

Flavored Meringue Cookie Recipe

Meringue cookies can be made to any flavor by adding flavored extract. You might have to experiment with extract amounts, though. Food color can make them fun colors to go with your flavors!

Ingredients:

1/4 teaspoon extract (orange, maple, lemon, almond ... whatever extract you want)
3 egg whites
1/8 teaspoon cream of tartar
3/4 cup granulated sugar.

Procedure:

Make sure egg whites are at room temperature.

Preheat oven to 250 degrees(F).

Combine egg whites, cream of tartar and extract. Beat until soft peaks are formed (about 4 or 5 minutes).

While still beating, slowly add sugar, then beat until mixture becomes glossy and stiff peaks are formed.

Push batter onto parchment-lined cookie sheet and put in oven on middle rack. Reduce heat to 200 degrees(F) at once. Bake for 25 to 30 minutes. Turn off oven and let it cool before removing cookies.

A Note From The Author

Thanks so much for reading, *"Mummified Meringues"*. I hope you liked reading it as much as I loved writing it. If you did, and feel inclined to leave a review, I really would appreciate it.

This is book ten of the USA Today best selling Lexy Baker series. I plan to write many more books with Lexy, Nans and the gang. I have several other series that I write, too - you can find out more about them on my website *http://www.leighanndobbs.com*.

Also, if you like cozy mysteries with ghosts, magic and cats, then you'll like my book *"Dead Wrong"* which is book one in the Blackmoore Sisters series. Set in the fictional, seaside town of Noquitt Maine, the Blackmoore sisters will take you on a journey of secrets, romance and maybe even a little magic. I have an excerpt from it at the end of this book.

This book has been through many edits with several people and even some software programs, but since nothing is infallible (even the software programs), you might catch a spelling error or mistake and, if you do, I sure would appreciate it if you let me know - you can contact me at: *lee@leighanndobbs.com*.

Oh, and I love to connect with my readers, so please do visit me on facebook at *http://www.facebook.com/leighanndobbsbooks*

Signup to get my newest releases at a discount:
http://www.leighanndobbs.com/newsletter

About The Author

Leighann Dobbs has had a passion for reading since she was old enough to hold a book, but she didn't put pen to paper until much later in life. After a twenty-year career as a software engineer with a few side trips into selling antiques and making jewelry, she realized you can't make a living reading books, so she tried her hand at writing them and discovered she had a passion for that, too! She lives in New Hampshire with her husband, Bruce, their trusty Chihuahua mix, Mojo, and beautiful rescue cat, Kitty.

Find out about her latest books and how to get discounts on them by signing up at:

http://www.leighanndobbs.com/newsletter
Connect with Leighann on Facebook and Twitter
http://facebook.com/leighanndobbsbooks
http://twitter.com/leighanndobbs

More Books By Leighann Dobbs:
Mystic Notch
Cat Cozy Mystery Series
* * *

Ghostly Paws
A Spirited Tail

Blackmoore Sisters
Cozy Mystery Series
* * *

Dead Wrong
Dead & Buried
Dead Tide
Buried Secrets
Deadly Intentions

Lexy Baker
Cozy Mystery Series
* * *

Lexy Baker Cozy Mystery Series Boxed Set Vol 1
(Books 1-4)

Or buy the books separately:

Killer Cupcakes
Dying For Danish
Murder, Money and Marzipan
3 Bodies and a Biscotti
Brownies, Bodies & Bad Guys
Bake, Battle & Roll
Wedded Blintz
Scones, Skulls & Scams
Ice Cream Murder

Kate Diamond
Adventure/Suspense Series

* * *

Hidden Agemda

Dobbs "Fancytales"
Regency Romance Fairytales Series
* * *

Something In Red
Snow White and the Seven Rogues
Dancing On Glass
The Beast of Edenmaine
The Reluctant Princess
Sleeping Heiress

Contemporary
Romance
* * *

Sweet Escapes
Reluctant Romance

***

Excerpt From Dead Wrong:

Morgan Blackmoore tapped her finger lightly on the counter, her mind barely registering the low buzz of voices behind her in the crowded coffee shop as she mentally prioritized the tasks that awaited her back at her own store.

"Here you go, one yerba mate tea and a vanilla latte." Felicity rang up the purchase, as Morgan dug in the front pocket of her faded denim jeans for some cash which she traded for the two paper cups.

Inhaling the spicy aroma of the tea, she turned to leave, her long, silky black hair swinging behind her. Elbowing her way through the crowd, she headed toward the door. At this time of morning, the coffee shop was filled with locals and Morgan knew almost all of them well enough to exchange a quick greeting or nod.

Suddenly a short, stout figure appeared, blocking her path. Morgan let out a sharp breath, recognizing the figure as Prudence Littlefield.

Prudence had a long running feud with the Blackmoore's which dated back to some sort of run-in she'd had with Morgan's grandmother when they were young girls. As a result, Prudence loved to harass and berate the Blackmoore girls in public. Morgan's eyes darted around the room, looking for an escape route.

"Just who do you think you are?" Prudence demanded, her hands fisted on her hips, legs spaced shoulder width apart. Morgan noticed she was wearing her usual knee high rubber boots and an orange sunflower scarf.

Morgan's brow furrowed over her ice blue eyes as she stared at the older woman's prune like face.

"Excuse me?"

"Don't you play dumb with me Morgan Blackmoore. What kind of concoction did you give my Ed? He's been acting plumb crazy."

Morgan thought back over the previous week's customers. Ed Littlefield *had* come into her herbal remedies shop, but she'd be damned if she'd announce to the whole town what he was after.

She narrowed her eyes at Prudence. "That's between me and Ed."

Prudence's cheeks turned crimson. Her nostrils flared. "You know what *I* think," she said narrowing her eyes and leaning in toward Morgan, "I think you're a witch, just like your great-great-great-grandmother!"

Morgan felt an angry heat course through her veins. There was nothing she hated more than being called a witch. She was a Doctor of Pharmacology with a Master Herbalist's license, not some sort of spell-casting conjurer.

The coffee shop had grown silent. Morgan could feel the crowd staring at her. She leaned forward, looking wrinkled old Prudence Littlefield straight in the eye.

"Well now, I think we know that's not true," she said, her voice barely above a whisper, "Because if I was a witch, I'd have turned you into a newt long ago."

Then she pushed her way past the old crone and fled out the coffee shop door.

***

Fiona Blackmoore stared at the amethyst crystal in front of her wondering how to work it into a pendant. On most days, she could easily figure out exactly how to cut and position the stone, but right now her brain was in a pre-caffeine fog.

Where was Morgan with her latte?

She sighed, looking at her watch. It was ten past eight, Morgan should be here by now, she thought impatiently.

Fiona looked around the small shop, *Sticks and Stones*, she shared with her sister. An old cottage that had been in the family for generations, it sat at one of the highest points in their town of Noquitt, Maine.

Turning in her chair, she looked out the back window. In between the tree trunks that made up a small patch of woods, she had a bird's eye view of the sparkling, sapphire blue Atlantic Ocean in the distance.

The cottage sat about 500 feet inland at the top of a high cliff that plunged into the Atlantic. If the woods were cleared, like the developers wanted, the view would be even better. But Fiona would have none of that, no matter how much the developers offered them, or how much they needed the money. She and her sisters would never sell the cottage.

She turned away from the window and surveyed the inside of the shop. One side was setup as an apothecary of sorts. Antique slotted shelves loaded with various herbs lined the walls. Dried weeds hung from the rafters and several mortar and pestles stood on the counter, ready for whatever herbal concoctions her sister was hired to make.

On her side sat a variety of gemologist tools and a large assortment of   crystals. Three antique oak and glass jewelry cases displayed her creations. Fiona smiled as she looked at them. Since childhood she had been fascinated with rocks and gems so it was no surprise to anyone when she grew up to become a gemologist and jewelry designer, creating jewelry not only for its beauty, but also for its healing properties.

The two sisters vocations suited each other perfectly and they often worked together providing customers with crystal and herbal healing for whatever ailed them.

The jangling of the bell over the door brought her attention to the front of the shop. She breathed a sigh of relief when Morgan burst through the door, her cheeks flushed, holding two steaming paper cups.

"What's the matter?" Fiona held her hand out, accepting the drink gratefully. Peeling back the plastic tab, she inhaled the sweet vanilla scent of the latte.

"I just had a run in with Prudence Littlefield!" Morgan's eyes flashed with anger.

"Oh? I saw her walking down Shore road this morning wearing that god-awful orange sunflower scarf. What was the run-in about this time?" Fiona took the first sip of her latte, closing her eyes and waiting for the caffeine to power her blood stream. She'd had her own run-ins with Pru Littlefield and had learned to take them in stride.

"She was upset about an herbal mix I made for Ed. She called me a witch!"

"What did you make for him?"

"Just some Ginkgo, Ginseng and Horny Goat Weed ... although the latter he said was for Prudence."

Fiona's eyes grew wide. "Aren't those herbs for impotence?"

Morgan shrugged "Well, that's what he wanted."

"No wonder Prudence was mad...although you'd think just being married to her would have caused the impotence."

Morgan burst out laughing. "No kidding. I had to question his sanity when he asked me for it. I thought maybe he had a girlfriend on the side."

Fiona shook her head trying to clear the unwanted images of Ed and Prudence Littlefield together.

"Well, I wouldn't let it ruin my day. You know how *she* is."

Morgan put her tea on the counter, then turned to her apothecary shelf and picked several herbs out of the slots. "I know, but she always seems to know how to push my buttons. Especially when she calls me a witch."

Fiona grimaced. "Right, well I wish we *were* witches. Then we could just conjure up some money and not be scrambling to pay the taxes on this shop and the house."

Morgan sat in a tall chair behind the counter and proceeded to measure dried herbs into a mortar.

"I know. I saw Eli Stark in town yesterday and he was pestering me about selling the shop again."

"What did you tell him?"

"I told him we'd sell over our dead bodies." Morgan picked up a pestle and started grinding away at the herbs.

Fiona smiled. Eli Stark had been after them for almost a year to sell the small piece of land their shop sat on. He had visions of buying it, along with some adjacent lots in order to develop the area into high end condos.

Even though their parents early deaths had left Fiona, Morgan and their two other sisters property rich but cash poor the four of them agreed they would never sell. Both the small shop and the stately ocean home they lived in had been in the family for generations and they didn't want *their* generation to be the one that lost them.

The only problem was, although they owned the properties outright, the taxes were astronomical and, on their meager earnings, they were all just scraping by to make ends meet.

All the more reason to get this necklace finished so I can get paid. Thankfully, the caffeine had finally cleared the cobwebs in her head and Fiona was ready to get to work. Staring down at the amethyst, a vision of the perfect shape to cut the stone appeared in her mind. She grabbed her tools and started shaping the stone.

Fiona and Morgan were both lost in their work. They worked silently, the only sounds in the little shop being the scrape of mortar on pestle and the hum of Fiona's gem grinding tool mixed with a few melodic tweets and chirps that floated in from the open window.

Fiona didn't know how long they were working like that when the bell over the shop door chimed again. She figured it must have been an hour or two judging by the fact that the few sips left in the bottom of her latte cup had grown cold.

She smiled, looking up from her work to greet their potential customer, but the smile froze on her face when she saw who it was.

Sheriff Overton stood in the door flanked by two police officers. A toothpick jutted out of the side of Overton's mouth and judging by the looks on all three of their faces, they weren't there to buy herbs or crystals.

Fiona could almost hear her heart beating in the silence as the men stood there, adjusting their eyes to the light and getting their bearings.

"Can we help you?" Morgan asked, stopping her work to wipe her hands on a towel.

Overton's head swiveled in her direction like a hawk spying a rabbit in a field.

"That's her." He nodded to the two uniformed men who approached Morgan hesitantly. Fiona recognized one of the men as Brody Hunter, whose older brother Morgan had dated all through high school. She saw Brody look questioningly at the Sheriff.

The other man stood a head taller than Brody. Fiona noticed his dark hair and broad shoulders but her assessment of him stopped there when she saw him pulling out a pair of handcuffs.

Her heart lurched at the look of panic on her sister's face as the men advanced toward her.

"Just what is this all about?" She demanded, standing up and taking a step toward the Sheriff.

There was no love lost between the Sheriff and Fiona. They'd had a few run-ins and she thought he was an egotistical bore and probably crooked too. He ignored her question focusing his attention on Morgan. The next words out of his mouth chilled Fiona to the core.

"Morgan Blackmoore ... you're under arrest for the murder of Prudence Littlefield."

Made in United States
Troutdale, OR
04/19/2024